Flush

Ivan Wayne Baker

Flush

By Ivan Wayne Baker

Three Faced Media

ISBN:147510765X
ISBN-13:9781475107654

DEDICATION

For Antoinette Jr. and Ivan IV

ACKNOWLEDGMENTS

For the support and the encouragement to realize dreams, I thank my wife and children, my parents and siblings, my friends and family. Special thanks to lifelong friend Daniel Warschkow who has been there throughout all creative endeavors, especially with editing and the artwork of this book. To Rory Klawien, Susana Roman and Hans Kurz, and John Vitek, much love and appreciation for all the support to make this first print happen.

The abdomen is the reason why man does not easily take himself as a God.

– Friedrich Nietzsche

Chapter 1: Toothbrush

I used a toothbrush to make myself vomit.

Some use their fingers or thumbs. Some use castor oil. Romans used feathers and sponges.

When you become bulimic, you find out that there are lots of interesting ways that get people to blow their chunks. I always stuck with my toothbrush. It serves two purposes, it started the whole mess and then it cleans your mouth when you're done. I carried mine in my back pocket.

Commonly, to make yourself vomit, you jam your hand so far back in your mouth that your teeth bruise the back of your hand. The toothbrush saves you the bruises, so people don't catch on to what you're doing. Eating disorders are deemed embarrassing. And the toothbrush also saves your teeth from rotting, so say mothers.

I figured it was a great idea to lose my lunch when I was being monitored for this exact thing at the Felicity Treatment Center. My mother sent me there for My Bulimia and Alcoholism and Anger.

After my first meal at the Felicity Treatment Center, there stood a counselor at the threshold of my room. He was there to guard me from myself and my disorder.

It was enough privacy to secretly purge. The plan was simple. Take a piss. Pretend to brush teeth with water running. Quick purge the food from the stomach into the toilet.

The first two steps went well. Unfortunately, the last one did not. Poor Charles Atkins, an honest hardworking grad student trying to put himself through school, was just doing the job he was paid peanuts to do.

He must have been suspicious when I was brushing my teeth with the water running full blast.

I caught a glimpse in the mirror of him rushing at me. It was too late. I turned to engage him and the vomit was already spewing forth, there was no way I could stop it once it started.

A putrid and steady flow of half-chewed bread and meat and vegetables was blasting on him and on me. He was relentless in trying to subdue me, quite dedicated to his lousy paying job.

He had me at first, both of his arms wrapped around me.

My first blast sprayed onto where our chests met. I had the courtesy to not puke directly in his face. The poor guy was just doing what the FTC barely paid him to do, work ethic.

Brave Charles, who had to take this kind of abuse for a measly 10 dollars an hour, didn't know ahead of time what he was getting into.

I had been wrestling since the 3rd grade. Common sense might have told him that boys aren't bulimic unless they're wrestlers or jockeys. I was too big to be a jockey. Back then, in suburban America, male bulimia was almost synonymous with wrestling.

He never expected that kind of resistance from a punk teenager, wrestler or not. Whatever he did or didn't anticipate, it didn't really matter, because after that initial blast of puke, I had regained my wits for long enough to throw him to the floor.

I lowered myself (what the coach called "taking a seat") enough to where he lost control of my arms. We called it a *bear hug*, others call it a *body hold*.

I felt like I was mud-wrestling but in place of mud it was my barely chewed and digested lunch. I was really surprised that he kept his own lunch down. As much as I was used to vomit and everything that it involved, this was still incredibly disgusting.

Before either of us could perform another wrestling move, we were dog-piled. And I got what was coming to me.

A large needle in one of my butt cheeks.

Chapter 2: Chicken Little

After the counselors subdued me, with manpower and a Thorazine injection, they strapped me to a gurney. They used giant ratchet straps like the ones that fasten ladders to vans.

They wheeled me into a room they called the *isolation room* for a period of what they called *quiet time*. Naturally I felt isolated and quiet. I thought about being strapped to a van.

The drugs kept intensifying, my heart rate slowed. Before fading out completely, I heard the counselors talking about the swaddles' on my legs.

They called those straps, *swaddles*, like we were babies that needed swaddling. Everything had a pleasant name. The name for this place my mom locked me in was the Felicity Treatment Center as if it was a happy place. In truth, it was a festering mess of teenage sorrow with no real solutions to offer. And the truth would come out.

Anything that had a negative connotation was given a kinder, gentler name. A violent act, like what I was involved in, was called a *conundrum* . Suicide attempts were called *accidents*.

The FTC wanted everyone subdued, in every way. Most of the staff sounded like robots, they were constantly saying "Everything is going to be okay, we promise". Of course it was, the drugs make it "okay". If electroshock therapy and lobotomies were legal again, the FTC would be turning out drones every minute. Calm and passive members of society. Status quo. More like sheep to the slaughter, unable to think critically and fight back.

Teenagers are naïve if anything. When your mother drives you to a place that will help you with your problems, you shrug, knowing you do have problems, and go along with the whole mess. If you knew what was coming, what was actually going on inside that Treatment Center or for others, The Military Academy, you might put up a fight much like a criminal resisting arrest. But without the knowledge and experience, you just go along with the whole charade. How bad can it be?

I did none of the talking on the way to the Felicity Treatment Center. My mom had been selling me on it all morning. She had been peddling me it like the Bible. She would do the same thing with Jesus after she found out that I didn't believe what she believed. Same way.

I had seen the FTC commercials. Teenagers were smiling and laughing, playing sports and making crafts. Some creepy synthesized music would be accompanied by a choir of high school angels, "A place to make friends. A place to get better." Over and over and over again. They had this corny slogan at the end of it, "If your child doesn't get better with us, please pray they get better somewhere".

I rarely had conversations with my mother during those awkward years. She would lecture or scold me and I would shrug and say "oh well".

Mom always had the Christian easy-listening station on, WCCA, W-Christ's Choir of Angels. Like the rest of the radio stations, the religious ones were littered with commercials. Nothing's sacred in Capitalism.

A McMill's commercial was on. McMill's was the largest fast-food chain in the entire universe, a proud subsidiary of Santomon which was one of the largest corporate conglomerates in all the cosmos. Half of all commercials were Santomon's in some way, shape, or form. It is quite possible that they owned half of the entire universe. If you bought a soda and a pack of smokes and filled your tank with gas, chances are that McMill's owned the companies that sold you those products.

This particular commercial was part of the new EnergyMill Burger ad campaign. It was narrated by a supposed astronaut. When he gets hungry out in space after a long hard day of working in the zero gravity cargo bay, he prefers to replenish himself with McMill's new EnergyMill Burger.

Yeah right. If he ate one of their burgers out in space, he'd fill his spacesuit with diarrhea. Everyone knew it, McMill's burgers make you shit yourself, yet people still eat their monstrous burgers.

My mom turned off the radio. Her voice was excited, she was driving fast.

"Do you want to get a burger before we get there?" She said.

I looked at her. She knew I didn't eat that crap.

We were at a stoplight. McMill's was on the corner. McMill's was on every fourth corner of every city in the world.

"This is for your own good Jacob. I'm paying a lot of money for this, money we don't really have. This isn't punishment. I just want you to be okay. We've suffered so much since your father left us. I know you inherited a lot of traits from that crazy blasphemer. The drinking and the anger. You definitely got that from your father. But the bulimia, I think you were born with that. That is God's trial for you. I should have never signed that wrestling waiver for your body fat. That just made it worse." Mom said.

I kept my mouth shut. I had nothing good to say. It was my honesty that got me into the situation in the first place. All I had to say was "no" when she asked me if I was bulimic, but then again I would have never met Ana. My gentle and beautiful and skinny idol, Ana.

"You used to make yourself puke when you were a toddler. You always had to have my attention. You would make yourself puke by sticking your finger down your throat. Our doctor said it wasn't a big deal, but look at you now. I think your bulimia is a disease, like your alcoholism is. I hope you can get healed. I pray for your soul every night. I wish you would accept Jesus into your heart. Father O'Leary is concerned about you. I wish you would have gone to see him, he could have helped you and we could have avoided this."

The more my mom talked, the more I wanted to be locked up in the FTC, to cease the endless lecturing.

***

I have a few memories of puking as a kid, but I have no recollection of self-induced purging before doing it for wrestling. I really had no reason to doubt my mom's story, aside for the fact that she should have been the one going for treatment.

We were at church carnival on a ride called *Spinsane*. This is the ride that spins so fast you stick to a movable vertical gurney which drifts upwards the faster it gets. A child's first glimpse at astronaut training, and I had no desire to be an astronaut after that.

We were spinning around with psychotic music playing, machine gun drums with a calliope of digital wind chimes. I remember not liking the sensation of my face peeling back and the lack of ability to move my arms from the wall. I felt nauseous but dealt with it.

Across from me at about 10 o'clock was an average woman looking green in the face. All at once, vomit came out, the inertia had prevented it from spewing *forth.* So the poor woman puked a fair amount of multicolored vomit all over the faces of her two neighbors and her own.

There wasn't a chain reaction of pukers to follow. This wasn't a Roman party. I struggled with the patience of a fearful boy to keep my stomach down, at least until I got outside to the 55-gallon garbage can which had already been used as a puke-bucket by many.

I let loose a flowing pink stream textured with chunks of bread and bologna, the results of the 80's American cold lunch, toxic red sugar beverage with a sandwich made from by-product meat and processed cheese and pesticidal veggies, the pesticides and vegetables of course manufactured by Santomon. No wonder everyone's so healthy.

There were a few other memories of others puking during my childhood. When my dad was working as a volunteer wildlife rescuer on the weekends, he took me with him sometimes. One rainy Saturday, he responded to a call about a swan. This large beautiful white bird was caught in barbed wire, my dad started clipping the wire far enough from a beak attack. He tried for nearly an hour to free it. Naturally the swan was angry and frantic, and as soon as my dad got too close, it puked at him, this would be its *swan song*. "The thing has suffered enough", my dad said, and he told me to turn around. I did what I was told. He shot it with his pistol.

He was truly bothered by the situation and didn't talk much for the rest of the day. Weeks later we had animal rights protesters outside of our house with signs that read "Swan Killer" or "Bird Murder". My father loved these kinds of situations, he loved confrontation. He stood on our lawn drinking beer and making his own signs. They read – "The End is Near" and below that "We're All Going To DIE". There was some shouting and chanting back and forth for several hours, but he ended up talking with each of the protestors, one by one until they left.

"What did you tell them?" My brother Cy had asked him.

My dad said. "The truth."

The worst personal memory of vomit was the last one I experienced until bulimia. My mother never brought that episode up, probably because it was her fault. I would never see the day when that woman would admit she wrong.

I was seven years old. My mother cooked us fried chicken for dinner. I loved fried chicken, or any chicken for that matter. I was struggling with eating a thigh piece, half my teeth were missing. I noticed a little pink flesh and didn't think twice about it. I didn't know what salmonella was. I thought it was a type of fish related to salmon. I found out the hard way that it's bacteria that makes you ill.

My guts were burning not long after dinner, and I went and hid in the bathroom, vomit and diarrhea went everywhere. It was out of my control, this poor kid could not contain any of this. I was so embarrassed and no one had seen the mess yet. I was trying to clean with my abdomen on fire. I couldn't think or see straight.

I don't know how long I was in there, but my parents and my brother caught on that there was something wrong. Here was this naked kid covered in shit and puke on the bathroom floor sobbing in pain.

My family took me to the hospital. The doctor told us that I had salmonella. This wasn't uncommon and not fatal for adults, but kids and the elderly can die from dehydration after days of puking and diarrhea.

I was bedridden for under a week. The first few days were a nightmare, my belly full of razors. The nurses gave me my nutrients and hydration through an IV.

My mom blamed it on the chicken. Bad batch or something. She could never admit that she didn't cook it thoroughly. I didn't blame her, it was an honest mistake, it happens all the time. I just wanted her to say sorry. It would take me going to hell and back for her to apologize for anything, and even with her apology, she would never admit she was wrong.

***

My father was an eschatologist and a functional alcoholic. He studied everything that had to do with the end of the world and drank too much. He justified his alcoholism as part of his belief system. He would often say, "Spirits for my spirit." He felt that alcohol kept him in touch with all of the gods inside himself, from the most animalistic to the most divine. "The Gods are inside me, and inside you," he often said.

"This stuff keeps me human, and it's a great antiseptic", he once said while holding up a bottle of homemade dandelion wine after he had just fell over from drunkenness.

Our family fell apart because of those two things. His fascination with the end of the world made him critical of the Abrahamic religions, more importantly Christianity via Roman Catholicism. He believed that the three major religions obsessed with End Time and Jerusalem always wanted to force Apocalypse. The Rebuilding of the Temple, the Second Coming, and Allah's Last Judgment. He felt that he had to be fanatical with preparing for their prophecy, because those three groups will, in his mind, make the world end.

He told me once, "this is because they were given the receipt of the world. They declare ownership, so they can do with it whatever they damn well pleased. This only means destroying this planet to get to heaven and go back to God".

With my mother being a devout Catholic, my father's alcoholism and outspokenness towards Christianity doomed their marriage and collapsed our family. For years she was patient with him, but there came a point when she realized that her praying was not going to get him to change or leave for that matter.

When me and my brother Cy were young, my dad would come home from the bar at two in the morning and wake us up. This was our Procedure of End Time Emergency Routine, or P.E.T.E.R. (as kids, Cy and I laughed at this, we called our penises *peters*). We were trained to make preparations to evacuate the city if civilization was quickly collapsing.

PETER was my father's forced acronym to represent Jesus' disciple Peter. Peter denied Jesus, and my dad said we would be denying the Second Coming so we can live in the world after civilization collapsed.

"The sky is falling! The sky is falling! Air raid, Air raid! The meteor has landed! Tsunami! Volcano! Earthquake! Get up you maggots and ready yourselves!" He would yell things like this. Me and Cy were made to do silly drills that didn't make much sense for evacuation, like doing push-ups and sit-ups and standing at attention. Every once in a while he'd have us stand at attention while he served us his favorite snack, limburger cheese and pickled herring on a cracker. We'd stand there, snack in hand, back straight and eyes forward. "Down the hatch!" He'd say.

Sometimes he would have us unpack and repack our Survival Rucksacks which were supposed to be ready at all times. He'd be blitzkrieg drunk while doing this. Most of the time, these middle-of-the-night drills were contradictory to what we had actually been trained while he was sober.

***

Every summer my dad took Cyrus and me on four or five day Survival Expeditions, our vacations. We went to different forest preserves with only our Survival Rucksacks which held the basics; tarp and mosquito net, knife and cord, very little food. Cy and I always snuck extra food, because if we didn't catch or kill enough wild game, we'd be starving by the last day. Our bellies were never satisfied with nuts and greens and mushrooms. My dad carried two extra items, a casket of whiskey (or some other homemade liquor) and a guitar he made while Cy was cooking in my mom's belly oven.

We had various tasks that were assigned to us throughout the day, but most of the time was spent hunting and foraging nuts, mushrooms, and other edibles. Every night, we sat around the fire telling jokes and stories and singing songs. My father had a particular favorite that he wrote himself called *Live in the World.*

If he was too drunk to play it right, Cy or I would take over. The song was easy, three chords.

Under the light of the moon and stars, behind tongues of flame, with me banging sticks and Cy playing guitar in time, my inebriated father sang and yelled over and over.

"Live in the world."

"Live in the world"

"Not the next."

***

My dad was forced to leave about a year before I went to the FTC. My mother's priest, Father O'Leary, came to the house and got him to leave, for good. It was the only time I had ever a seen priest get angry and ready to defend himself physically. Father O'Leary came from Boston and was known for his boxing and his occasional pint of stout. No violence came of the situation, just my dad yelling insults about Christianity.

"You know that the Devil only exists inside of you, he's not this invisible demon that you make your sheep so afraid of. You're no saint. You're human like the rest of us." My father yelled at Father O'Leary. They had a history.

"I am no saint! And I'll show you how human I am", said the priest.

He took off his cassock and removed his clerical collar.

Father O'Leary and my dad were in boxing stances. My mother was screaming at them both to stop.

I watched in awe. I did not want to mix it up with my two fathers regardless of wrestling knowledge.

My father gave up. He sobered from the excitement. He grabbed his duffle bag and before leaving said. "Don't ever forget everything I taught you Jacob, you'll be a survivor. People like Father O'Leary and your mother *want* the world to end so they can be with their God and chosen people in heaven. I trained you to survive their planetary destruction so you can live in this world. I'll write you when I can, son."

And he did. He wrote me once a month from Alaska. He lived like a mountain man on a commune with like-minded people making wine and liquor to barter with townsfolk for supplies . I never wrote back.

In one of his letters, he wrote how people were condemning him and his little band of eschatologists. The media was calling them "terrorists" and "extremists".

Some of what he wrote:

I'm no terrorist Jacob. The shit the government had me do in Vietnam was enough terrorism for a man's life time. I never want to see that again. I just want to co-exist with nature, and they think that is extreme. They'll see when everything collapses then they'll know. They'll never believe people like us until they are starving, thirsty, and desperate.

If you tire of that life, the hustle and bustle of our lunatic society, come see me.

I'm sorry for not being around. You always have a place up here.

Love, your father

I regret never writing him back. He never held it against me.

My mother forgave him for everything but refused to read his letters to her. She may have never admitted fault for anything, but she practiced what she preached about forgiveness in Christianity.

***

My arrival to Felicity Treatment Center was staged to be a smooth transfer. It was nothing of the sort. I was a gullible teenager who had no idea of what was coming. My mom hugged me and choked back tears. I couldn't hug her back. I had realized that this was a sham.

My mom talked to the receptionist who then sent for someone to check my backpack.

This was the Survival Rucksack that I was raised with. Instead of a knife and tarp and rope there were four sets of plain and fitted clothes. (Rule #21 All clothing must be void of words or images) and (Rule #22 No loose or tight clothing.)

The reinforced steel doors alerted me to the fact that this was a place where they intended you to stay until they fixed you. It wasn't exactly what the pamphlet and commercials had portrayed, a fun place where I could meet good looking girls like the ones in the commercial. But I did get to meet the best looking girl that I would ever come to know.

The clunks of the automated locks were loud and threatening, and to a punk kid who's indefinitely confined, it's very miserable.

They send you through those doors like near-death survivors to the white light, a point-of-no-return. "Hi" and "Hello" and "Welcome", the counselors were paid peanuts to smile.

I saw some action through a window, counselors were smiling as they were restraining a screaming and crying girl. She was yelling like an archetypal crazy person, but what she was saying was serious. "My elbow is broken." My counselors ignored it and escorted me down to the orientation room.

They sat me at a long table in front of a TV and played an orientation video about the Felicity Treatment Center. The jingle of their commercial played during the introduction, but unlike the commercial, the video showed me how miserable we all are and how they intend to fix that. There were clips of teenagers crying in their bedrooms hugging themselves to sleep. There was a kid with razorblades in a steamy shower, a girl drinking from a bottle of bleach, a guy tying a noose. "Life doesn't have to be like this", written in big bold scrolling letters down the screen. Felicity Treatment Center is a proud subsidy of Proxy and Keno, the biggest pharmaceutical company on the planet.

Much like the commercial, everyone was smiling and cured, then some words from their sponsors which consisted of advertisements for the new medications that bring *happiness*. Side effects included oily discharge, nausea, stomach pains, et cetera.

The counselors offered me refreshments and snacks. I declined. I was terribly hungry, but I didn't know if I could puke anytime soon.

After the orientation video was finished, they took me to the next door down. Here was the session with the psychiatrist. I expected to be laid down on a fainting couch. I didn't know the difference between a psychiatrist and a psychologist.

I soon found out that a psychiatrist is someone ordained to classify your insanity. After that is established, the psychiatrist decides a method of treatment, in most case they prescribe medication to fix you. At the FTC, it wasn't a matter of whether or not you were crazy, it was a question of which crazy are you.

The counselors put me in a room the size of a janitor's closet and told me to fill out a test. I was tempted to fill in the bubbles (A through E) with silly words like BABE or CAB or BAD, but I was curious about the content of the questionnaire and couldn't help being honest.

Some of the expected questions read like this:

1."How often do you get angry?

Very Often /Often /Sometimes /Seldom /Never

2.How often do you think about killing yourself?

Very Often /Often /Sometimes /Seldom /Never

3.Do you drink or take drugs with consideration that you might die from it?

Very Often /Often /Sometimes /Seldom /Never

4.Do you eat in the middle of the night?

Very Often /Often /Sometimes /Seldom /Never

And so on.

I took my time with each question, considering each one carefully. By the hundredth question, I was barely reading and answering only with *sometimes* or *seldom*. This would prove to be a mistake since one of the questions read: “Do you ever consider killing your parents?”

I was escorted into a spacious office and greeted by the psychiatrist.

Dr. Bauer was an attractive 30 year-old brunette who had the entire universe figured out, with me being no exception.

I had her figured out.

She was probably divorced if she had ever gotten married in the first place. She reminded me of all those girls at my school who couldn’t or wouldn’t keep a steady boyfriend due to their principles of achievement. They were too strong for their own good, and I was the one with an emotional suppression problem.

“Have a seat.” Dr. Bauer said and gestured to the chair across from her. I refrained from offering my hand for a shake because the desk was abnormally large.

I sat down and looked around. Dr. Bauer sat motionless except for her eyes.

“So.” Long pause. “Do you think you are an angry person?” She said.

“I don’t think so. I do get angry, but doesn’t everyone?” I made sure to make eye contact whenever I spoke. My father taught me this, an invaluable tool when dealing with authority figures.

Almost everything she asked me was already in the questionnaire. Occasionally she would scribble something and respond with "hmmm" or "interesting".

"Do your parents love you?" She asked.

"Of course."

"Interesting." She scribbled. "And you sometimes have thoughts of killing your parents?"

"No, of course not." I felt a bit panicked.

"Okay." She scribbled some more and pressed a button on the office phone. "We're finished now."

Chapter 3: I'm okay - You're Okay

Dr. Joseph Pavlovich was a psychologist, not a psychiatrist. He greeted me at the door, shook my hand, and invited me to have a seat.

"So what's the difference between you and a psychiatrist?"

He told me that a psychiatrist is a medical doctor and that he was not, he could not prescribe medication.

He sat in front of a wall of books behind an ancient desk. He paged through My Charts, or the FTC's version of who I was. He tossed them aside uninterested.

"Jacob, here's the deal. That silly questionnaire you just filled out. They've diagnosed you with Histrionic Personality Disorder. Are you familiar with this disorder?"

"No. How did they diagnose me so fast? I just took that test."

"I know. That's how things work these days. Don't worry though. I'm trying to waive your medication due to your disorder which is a good thing, but you will have to come see me three times a week instead of once per week with medication."

The mnemonic device used to diagnose Histrionic Personality disorder is PRAISE ME which explained how I was a self-centered attention monger, an egotistical maniac, a narcissist. Narcissus turned into a flower after looking at his image too long.

Dr. Pavlovich was a radical in his field. He was able to work for the FTC, because they hire anyone with a PhD in psychology to do therapy. Same with counselors, anyone who was old enough and willing to deal with mentally-twisted teenage brats for ten bucks an hour had themselves a job at the FTC.

They probably figured Dr. Pavlovich was desperate for a job, since he was fired from the last two universities for teaching outside the curriculum, and his personal practice was ridiculed by many shrinks despite his credentials. The FTC usually hired people freshly graduated with PhD's and with little or no experience, because they paid little for that profession. But at the FTC, a psychiatrist could earn commission with prescribing pharmaceuticals.

At one university long ago, Dr. Pavlovich rewrote the curriculum for a lower level psychology course without getting it approved. He was newly graduated and full of pep.

He asked the class, a lecture hall of a hundred plus students, if they bought Thomas A. Harris' book *I'm OK – You're OK*. He ordered those that raised their hands to go get a refund. He wasn't going to teach that book. "That's not how it goes." He was waving the book around like contraband. "I'm okay, you're okay'? No, no, no. It's 'I'm okay and you're all a bunch of assholes'. That's how it goes in our society." He tossed the book at the blackboard and started going through everything he was going to teach them.

Some perturbed students told on him. That was the last class he taught at that university.

Working for the FTC was actually his secret mission, not just a measly paycheck. He was on a mission to expose pharmaceutical companies that were using treatment centers and psychiatry to push their pills. He was a psychologist, so he didn't earn any pill payola like the psychiatrists. Regardless of his mission, he still took the patients seriously. He genuinely cared about a person's well being. The FTC gave him many liberties to treat patients with his own methods for which he was thankful, but all the while he internally investigated the

FTC's procedures. He was one of many in his radical group SAP, Shrinks Against Pharmacies. They would compile enough evidence to expose the mistreatment of patients at facilities nationwide. SAP would also reveal the connections between these pharmaceutical companies and treatment centers and how they used the centers to push their drugs at maximum prices. The public would be outraged for a day and then it was business as usual.

During my stay at FTC I never felt that Dr. Pavlovich was counseling me. I learned later that he had many different ideas on how to help someone's mind.

"Three times a week may seem like a lot, but trust me...it'll be fine. I'm not here to poke, prod, and probe you. I'll just treat you like a human being, and work on getting you release from this place." Dr. Pavlovich said.

He handed me a book-- *Heal Yourself.*

"That's just a dust cover so the counselors don't confiscate it. The book is actually *Dr. Mantha's Compendium of Myth and Legend.* Dr. Mantha is one of my friends and colleagues. Myth is a great tool to find ourselves. I figured you might have an interest in Greek and Roman culture since you're a wrestler."

I expected something different from a psychologist. I was waiting for all the questions about my mother and father and other cliché psychology questions. I thought he would hypnotize me on the fainting couch and make my inner child blather on about all the scary things of my youth, but there was none of that. To Dr. Pavlovich, I was a person, not a paycheck.

Chapter 4: Meal Caution

For what felt like an hour, passed eight. I was pacified and cozy, swaddled like a baby, and my mental state was reduced to just that, infancy.

The counselors unswaddled me and lifted me to my feet. Baby's first steps. Groggy and numb, I did the Thorazine shuffle with the counselors chaperoning me down porcelain white hallways.

I was being flushed down the FTC, the labyrinthine toilet, the pristine mask over unwanted shit. I was a wretched up blob of human waste floating along with the help of my toilet-water counselors down into the underworld of the secret sewage hell, into a place where no one has to deal with me anymore.

Not my mom, not my dad, not anyone important.

The Felicity Treatment Center was nothing more than the hybrid monstrosity you would get if Jails could procreate with Hospitals and allow their offspring to care for your troubled teens.

In the FTC, we could not be trusted. We could not be ourselves, be natural. We were tornadoes and thunderstorms, unwanted acts of nature.

I shuffled along in my lace-less shoes. I was put on Suicide Watch, not to be confused with the more intense Suicide Warning.

The FTC puts all their new patients on Suicide Watch. (Rule #33: All patients on Suicide Watch must be stripped of all potentially harmful items).

There were plenty of other things for you to harm yourself with, such as pencils and locks-in-socks and bed sheets, but those were overlooked for reasons unknown.

A few months prior to my arrival, a boy made a noose out of a bed sheet and he hanged himself. My roommate Allen was the one who found him there, swaying from a pipe above the drop-ceiling. According to Allen, the hanged kid's face was blue, his tongue out. Allen was still freaked out by the time I got there.

My head was flopping about like a limp puppet, and I was entranced by the dotted line of lights on the ceiling. Everything was sterilized with ultra-power-omnicidal-cleaner, which smelled of artificial strawberries, and colored of different tints of white. The brightest white was shaded by other not-so-bright whites. It reminded me of heaven, how there would have to be contrast with everything so bright and pure, like a cloud. But then there's Antarctica. White does not always mean goodness. These white places look pristine, but they are not paradises. They're hells to some, places of torment from which you can't escape until you've been whipped into shape.

We arrived at another set of clunky security doors and waited for the counselor in the central control station to open them.

The counselors checked me in at the nurse's station which was little more than a desk. It was located at the end of the day room. A male counselor and a female nurse stood behind an oversized podium that looked like a flight panel. I was looking dumbly at the surroundings and all my peers were looking dumbly back at me, peas in a pod.

A female nurse, corpulent and middle-aged, took My Charts from one of the counselors and wrote something on an index card. I noticed my mug shot and saw that my cheeks were fuller than I had expected. I must have gained a few pounds in the last few days. I had been eating and boozing too much.

I was pinching one of my cheeks unconsciously when I realized the nurse was talking to me.

"Fresh linens and a care-package are on your bed. Dinner is in ten minutes. Dorm number 4 Bed 2. This is for your footlocker." She was handing me a lock and a piece of paper. I couldn't concentrate. I was thinking about what a care-package meant, and I was awkwardly staring at the extra side-lumps of flesh bulging through her pukey green scrubs.

"Jacob…Jacob!"

Five fingers waved in my face.

"Yeah, sorry," I said, "it's the drugs they gave me." I pointed at my head and looked her in the face.

"I know. Here's your lock and combination. Now go get ready. Dinner's in ten minutes."

I nodded and did the Thorazine shuffle through the day room to my dorm.

The dorms and the day room were set up like cookie-cutter motel suites. There were two separate wings, one for each gender. (Rule #13: No patient shall enter the wing of their opposite sex.) Each wing had a dozen rooms. Each room had double beds with nightstands and bathroom. Each bathroom was equipped with sink, shower, and toilet. Above the sink was a plastic safety mirror. Far from accurately reflecting one's face, these mirrors were little more than funhouse mirrors. This is problematic when dealing with teenagers with every issue and insecurity in the book.

Everything was made to look and feel like home but tactically designed to keep the residents from harming themselves or each other. Blue argyle grandma couches were L-shaped for viewing the TV suspended in the corner. The table and chair sets along the one wall were rubbery plastic and primary colored, no sharp edges.

When I got to my room, my new roommate was reading in his bed. He either didn't hear me shuffle in or he didn't want to acknowledge me. I wasn't interested in meeting him either. I just sat on the bed and looked through my care-package. Little versions of everything in your bathroom, again just like a motel. The toothbrush was smaller than my first one. Chuck must have seen me use it to puke. Whatever. There were other ways, fingers and such. I didn't know how I could brush my teeth with the tiny thing let alone trigger a purge without swallowing it.

About a minute later, the nurse called us for chow time. I sluggishly made my way to the chow line, trying to avoid knocking into people. Half of these kids were shuffling around like me, drugged cattle. Everyone was trying to form some sort of line at the nurse's station. They're all stripped of their fashion accessories, but there was no mistaking what their chosen sub-culture was. A punk rocker or skater, hippy or goth, prep or gangster, or a mixture of all the above. I was spaced out so I couldn't concentrate on one person or thing. We were floating in line, two steps here and there, bobbing like half-chewed bits of food in the FTC stomach. The counselors who joined us Eating Disorders, or ED's, were the enzymes that carried us through the FTC's digestive process.

Besides being called ED's, anyone with an eating disorder had several specialized titles and nicknames, but we were called Meal Cautions by the staff during the entire eating procedure.

My counselor Robert had a nametag. He could've easily wrestled at the 189 lbs weight class if he shed 15 lbs or so, otherwise he would be at Heavyweight, 200 lbs and up. His midriff was a tad pudgy and he carried a lot in his face. The baggy white scrubs could only hide so much. He introduced himself as "Robert" and didn't start the small talk.

There was idle chatter among the patients about the upcoming meal. I started pinching my cheeks, wondering why the facial cheeks aren't a part of the body fat percentage test. I was still doped up. The Thorazine wouldn't let up. My stomach was empty and ravenous, and on the contrary I felt pukey.

We were tromping down the hallways, the cattle down the chute towards hay and oats. Or better yet, like floating cartoon dogs sleep-flying towards their nemesis' deliciously evil cauldron of stew. I couldn't have been hungrier. My stomach-rumbles were raucous and audible.

Welcome to High School Cafeteria, U.S.A. We all grabbed pre-prepped trays and sat in supposedly arbitrary places. (Rule #11: Cliques are not allowed in the FTC.) I was delighted and ravenous and tore into the meal.

I was a food fanatic and a wannabe chef. Eating and cooking were my obsessions. Everywhere you hear "You are what you eat.," I was everything.

I dug into the entrée, real beef stroganoff, and shoveled it in my mouth with a slow rhythm, the Thorazine made me sluggish and careless. Bits of food found their way out of my mouth corners.

The noodles were done to a perfect *al dente*, the mushrooms and almonds were between tender and firm, and the cream sauce had a nice trace of red wine vinegar. The mashed potatoes were real and creamy, topped with a sweet cream butter. As far as the FTC pamphlet went, they were right on about the food.

Food was my problem. And I found one solution, bulimia. Every time I ate I would imagine the food and the fat going straight under my skin and between my muscles as these lipid layers. This is the fat you can feel when you pinch your tummy or one of your triceps and guess your body fat percentage. I was always compulsively pinching my belly fat. At my very worst, I had bruises next to my belly button.

I shamelessly finished my food before everyone else even at my laggard pace. I sat there sipping my milk, involuntarily belching and looking around. There was a commotion at the end of my table. A girl was grunting and trying to get her arms back while two counselors enclosed her.

The girl was lanky. Her skin was the color of heavy whipping cream. She had cherry-plumped lips and a delicate nose. Her eyes were like two perfect scoops of Blue Moon ice cream in fine white china. Her cheekbones jutted out and cheeks sunk in. Her hair was straight and shaded with faded colors like an array of fresh spices - cayenne red, turmeric yellow, and basil green.

She went from anger to bawling in an instant. The counselors were talking to her in low altruistic voices while one held her arms and the other started shoving food in her mouth. She was shaking and sobbing. If she wasn't so frail, I thought she would be able to break free.

She cringed after each bite. She was salting her meal with tears and held each mouthful in for a few moments before taking one big swallow. She was beautiful in crying, and I thought everyone was ugly when they cried.

"Stop staring." Robert scolded. "And you have to slow down when you eat. You'll offend the ones that have a hard time eating, and you'll provoke those that like to eat too much."

"Sorry Bob." I looked at him with a finger to my head. "I usually eat a lot faster than that. The drugs made me slow."

Chapter 5: Chunks

In the dayroom, it was only us Meal Cautions, or ED's once our meal monitoring was over. Counselors sat by each of us, Robert next to me on a rubber couch.

The new girl was off in a corner with some female counselor who was having a serious talk with her. The new girl wasn't crying, she was calm and frustrated. Because of the facial distortion that comes with crying, I didn't *really* know how she looked. I kept staring over at her, soaking up her face.

She had a beautiful angular face, high cheek bones, sharp nose and plump lips. She definitely had the looks of a waif model. I didn't believe in the mythical *love at first sight,* but she had the beauty that I knew would never bore me.

Eating disorder or not, she had been thin her whole life and was made fun of for it. The mean kids in middle school might have called her Olive Oyl or Skeletor or Mary Carpenter. My half-Jewish friend David would've called her a Concentration Camper. This was what he called himself when he hadn't eaten in days after running away from home. He'd point at the self-given number tattoos on his forearm, the same numbers forced on his grandparents who were locked up in World War II, and say "I was 'camping'."

I couldn't stop looking over at her. I wanted so bad to meet her.

"Jacob, stop staring!" Robert said.

I glanced back at the TV and then to the girl again like a nosy little kid.

"Sorry Bob. She's cute. A lot cuter now that she's not crying and getting mashed potatoes stuffed in her mouth." I glanced again. Who was I fooling? She was the most beautiful girl, even in such an undignified condition. Robert just shook his head and gave up.

As a recipe, she consisted of a handful of different sub-cultural ingredients. She was a waif-model dessert made from a cup of Punk and a cup of Goth with a couple tablespoons of Hippy sprinkled on top.

I couldn't really tell, because her make-up had run so badly that she could have been a number of sub-cultures. She wouldn't be able to fix her make-up though. (Rule #17: No facial beauty products.)

I felt self-conscious once I realized what I was wearing. My mom made me pack normal clothes like the stuff you wear to church or family functions. I was like her, a jumbled mess of sub-cultures, of course in the original and unique style fashioned by myself and the group of friends I hung out with. In the FTC, I was Joe Jock American with a skater haircut, a chunk of longish hair on top of a shaved head. Outside the FTC, I was a walking thrift store with an undersized shirt and oversized pants.

The counselors only monitored us for twenty minutes which was supposedly enough to digest enough of a meal. The FTC had this to a science, literally. Some of their rehabilitation was to educate kids with eating disorders to become aware of the dangers, same with alcohol and drugs and anger.

So it wasn't but five minutes after the rest of the kids were released from their rooms did Robert let me alone. If I would have been a little more patient before, I wouldn't have had to go through the puke-wrestling bout with Chuck. My belly still felt full and undigested. I waited another five minutes for good measure.

I was then on my knees over the toilet with the shower running.

***

Regardless of any scientific truth there might be with digestion according to the FTC, I figured that if I half-chewed my food, it would have to take longer to digest.

I often thought of pythons and how they swallow whole rats. The rat in the python's belly eternally sleeps, slowly digesting.

So after that first day, the half-hour lag time after meals didn't bother me much. Puking up big chunks on the other hand wasn't as easy as regular puking.

My index and middle finger were as far in my mouth as I could fit them. I had to actually stroke my uvula to provoke the gag reflex. I contemplated using the wee brush in my care package but then I just forced my hand with a little more strength.

A couple dry heaves later, I was upchucking.

It didn't flow in a steady stream like normally chewed food. It was choppy and violent.

So I knelt at the toilet. It was pristine and polished. I looked at the chunks and thought about the view of the inside of my stomach.

I always have this moment of clarity after purging that leads me into rumination, like a sacred cow contemplating existence chewing on cud, or a monk coming back from the top of a mountain.

The toilet is the place for all human waste, consumed and ejected in some way or other. This is a place for asses and faces. It is a symbol for all those places that society has built to keep its waste.

People are like food in society. We're prepped with years of slicing and spicing and cooking to perfection, just to be consumed by an indifferent system. Some of us are McMill burgers and some *filet mignon*.

Chapter 6: Purging

Bulimia happened overnight, or so I thought. According to the FTC, I had been bulimic for years, with what they call non-purging *bulimia nervosa.* The purging kind though, was overnight. Or so I thought, all those laxatives I took to shit myself clean, were another form of purging style bulimia.

Watching my weight was a new concept to me during my Junior season. In grade school and middle school, I wrestled at my natural weight. In high school, weight doesn't become an issue until you're at the Varsity level. This became an issue for me during my sophomore year.

The best wrestlers are usually positioned at their natural weight class. This is determined by a wrestle-off. The better man gets the spot and the loser fills in where needed. Some guys are below weight and have nothing to worry about except a bigger opponent. The others have to sign medical release forms if they end up having to wrestle below 7% body fat.

At the beginning of my Sophomore season, the school's physical trainer came to give everyone a skin fold test. They use a caliper to measure your fat fold on your abdomen, triceps, and subscapular or your upper back fat. They put these in an equation with your bone density. If your target weight class requires you to be under 7%, your parents must sign a medical release for. My mother signed such a form and somehow blames this all on me.

I was wrestling at my natural weight, 145 lbs. at the Junior Varsity level when the guy at 140 lbs. broke his ankle. The coaches asked me to wrestle in his place. I was honored. I took on all the demands of being a Varsity wrestler.

When you have a match coming, you weigh yourself at least ten times a day, when you wake up and go to sleep, after you piss or shit, before practice, after practice, and any compulsive time you might feel the need to know. You count all your calories. Every day you shave and keep your hair and nails short. You trim your pubes because it all adds up. You chew tobacco on the bus ride to a tournament or meet, because the water weight of the saliva adds up. It gets that bad, that obsessive. At the scale every ounce counts. An ounce can prevent that lever on the scale from dropping.

I was terrible at fasting. Every Survival Expedition that my brother and I went on with my dad left us hungry. There was a lesson in starving about self-sufficiency and tolerance of misery that my dad intended for us to learn, but I never did then. I learned that I didn't like my belly empty.

A lot of guys in my wrestling squad had no problems eating nothing but a piece of fruit two or three days before a match. I couldn't do it. I would get home from a three-hour practice to a home-cooked meal. How could I resist? When she had the time, my mom was an excellent cook. To get rid of that weight, I jogged, jumped rope, and swam. Non-purging *bulimia nervosa.* It didn't work for me. Not only did it drain me of all my energy, I failed to make weight once.

***

It comes down to ounces. The spit in your mouth, the hair on your head.

During the beginning of my Junior-year season, I was struggling to make weight at every weigh-in. I had grown in height from the year before so I figured wrestling at 145 lbs instead of 140 lbs was completely reasonable. It didn't work out to be.

After the results from the first body fat test, I had to have my mom sign a medical waiver to go under the 7% body fat limit. I started the season weighing a natural 150 lbs, but the coach wanted me to wrestle at 140 lbs again. Those 10 lbs proved to be insanely difficult to keep off using the non-purging method.

The first few wrestling meets were nerve-racking, barely a hair worth of space would appear between the lever and the window it floats in. It's called a Physician Balance Beam Scale. I had planned to buy one for my house but couldn't save 200 bucks for it. The little shitty ones that everyone keeps in their bathroom aren't ever calibrated correctly. Who knows if you're 5 lbs over or under? Serious business for a wrestler.

At weigh-ins, two or three referees stand behind the scale. They start with the lowest weight class, 103 lbs, and end with the heavyweights.

You get on the scale with your hands out, palms down to check the length of your nails. They inspect your facial hair to make sure you're clean shaven. If you're one of those whose facial hair grows faster than grass then you'll have to shave again. They also do a quick inspection of your body to make sure you don't have *scabies*, *ringworm*, or any other contagious skin fungus. Generally everyone weighs in nude unless you're one of those who are confidently under weight.

During the weigh-ins of my first two Varsity matches, the end of the lever in that little metal window had created a small space and then closed the space and opened up again. My hands were out for the nail-check, shaking nervously. As a child, I used to get nervous because of my tough-looking opponent or just the match itself, but in those times, my weight had become the frightening foe.

I had barely ounced by in those first two weigh-ins. I lost both matches by points. I was perpetually fatigued. I fell asleep in class most of the time. I'd nod off and wake up startling myself, sometimes the teacher would do the startling.

My third match at Varsity level was the first and last time I failed to make weight.

It was the night before the match against Pine River. I was at the local gym later than usual. I managed to engorge myself with mom's casserole. It wasn't like it was her usual superb cuisine, just an in-a-hurry meal. I couldn't stop myself from getting one small serving after another and another and another. Small portions don't mean anything if you have a ton of them.

It takes twenty minutes for your brain to register that you are full. I had never sat and ate for twenty minutes in my whole life unless I was forced to. After those twenty minutes, when your belly is a bubbling blob, you want to go to sleep. Your mind is solving problems that your body hasn't yet. Whether you're starved or engorged, your mind releases endorphins to make you feel elated during pain. This is your body's back up plan for when the world ends, same plan as when it began.

I had nothing but distilled water all day, or what a bodybuilder friend of mine called Ethiopian Water Soup. Bodybuilders drink distilled water to dehydrate themselves for performance. Wrestlers drink it for fast weight loss. It's effective yet dangerous. Schools eventually started having hydration tests along with the body fat tests to prevent wrestlers from dehydrating themselves to death to make weight.

When I got home after wrestling practice, I devoured half the casserole dish. I was fatigued and my belly was protruding. I had to take a nap. I woke up two hours later at 8 o'clock and rushed to the gym.

I ran and I swam lethargically, feeling nauseous the entire time. I had to cut down much of the workout since the place closed at 10. To make up for the lost time, I thought it was a good idea to stay an extra five minutes in the steam room.

Before I ever had to cut weight, I wore a tank top and shorts. When keeping weight down, I wore a mandatory two layers, sweatpants and hooded sweatshirt covered with the wrestling team sweat-suit which was insulated.

After I was done swimming, I thought it was a good idea to go in the steamroom with my sweat-suit on, hood up and tightened. I was sitting on the tile bench watching the clock through the eucalyptus mist. I gave myself 15 minutes before I would have to get out of there.

I woke up with a gym janitor dragging me.

"Hey man, I had to get to you out of there!" The guy was serious.

I grumbled something. I got up, barely standing, he helped me.

I was confused and unsure of what was going on or where I was. The janitor had put my arm around his shoulder half-carrying me like in a war movie. He walked me through the eucalyptus cloud to the light.

I tried regaining my senses but was too dehydrated.

"You okay man?" The guy sat me down on a bench.

"Yeah, I think so." It was hard to look at the guy, I was in vertigo and embarrassed.

"Good. I figured something was wrong when a half hour had passed. I would've found you anyway since we're shutting down pretty soon. But really guy, that's dangerous being dressed up like that in that heat." He said.

I didn't say much, just thanked him and started changing. I had a strange sensation in my chest, somewhere between panic and elation. The more I thought about it, the scarier the situation was to me.

Next day, I was on the scale, hands out shaking, in front of the three refs, critical like underworld judges. The bald one was flicking the sub-marker from 39 to 39 1/2 to 40 and so on. At 40 the lever was still flush with the top of that window. I was panicked, the time crawled. He flicked it all the way to 41 and a little gap appeared.

"One hundred and forty six." The bald ref told the big ref with the clipboard. "You got a half hour bud. Better get your rope out."

I was crushed – feeling like a girlfriend dumped me or a boss fired me. I seriously wanted to cry and run home. I knew I wasn't going to shed that pound in an hour. My guts were emptied, already shitted out from the laxative chocolate. I spat until my mouth turned to desert again. My bladder depleted.

While everyone else was mowing down snacks, I was bundled up in three layers running the stairs and jumping rope alternately. I felt like passing out or dying, one seemed the same as the other. If I did make weight, I was extremely fatigued and would have been pinned in the first thirty seconds.

Half an hour later, my coach stood next to the scale with his hand on his chin in deep contemplation. The bald referee was behind scale in a permanent sigh. I stood there naked, a muscular heap of exhaustion, on the scale.

We all stared at the metal bar, it jiggled like it wanted to float free from the frame. It jiggled because of my shaking, I couldn't control it. My spirit kept me standing and staring at the metal bar, I was telepathically trying to move it. I thought it would be free. No such luck. I wasn't telepathic and I couldn't remove that last ounce with magic. It would take a knife to remove actual flesh to make weight.

But I didn't owe Shylock, The Merchant of Venice, my pound of flesh, though I would've gladly given it. I wanted to give my blood, slice my arm open and offer the judges my sacrificial ounce.

We were there for eternal minutes staring at the thing. My coach, with hand on chin, never moved. I exhaled as much out of my lungs as I could, thinking that the air weighed something. It weighed nothing.

The bald judge shrugged.

He said "Sorry kid."

I went deep in the locker room and pounded on the lockers. I screamed cusses and stomped my feet. A child's temper tantrum.

I was thinking about quitting wrestling all together and about the coach's and the team's disappointment and about my father not being around anymore to support me and my mother's hatred for him that she took out on me.

I was making strong grimaces to fight back the crying. My eyes welled up anyway and I half sobbed. I couldn't think about eating that turkey and cheddar sandwich sitting in my duffel bag. Then I got a pat on the back.

"Hey Jake, it's alright man, don't sweat it. It happens. Remember last year. I didn't make weight twice." It was Mike Borden, senior and team captain, 135 lbs., all around nice guy. He sat down next me.

"What do I have to do though? It's hard for me to fast so I make up for it by going to the gym after I eat." I sounded desperate and whiny. Not my father's son in those moments.

"I know how you feel. I have that same problem. I like to cook a lot so naturally I like to eat. I suggest that you start throwing up after you eat. Right after, so it doesn't digest." He said it so normally.

"That really works?"

I had heard of guys going 'bulimic', but I had never considered it as a real option.

"It works for me. I get the satisfaction of eating all my favorite foods and keeping weight. The puking part is weird at first, but you get used to it," he said.

Not only was Mike a great wrestler, he could cook like a champ. He hosted an end of the season dinner at his house. He served five courses for twenty of us, some of the best food I've ever eaten. If you like watching pigs feed, I suggest you watch twenty wrestlers have dinner after three months of starvation.

Mike taught me all the ins and outs of purging style *bulimia nervosa*, such as not chewing for too long, to carry a little bottle of mouthwash around so my teeth don't rot out, to be careful about pulling muscles from excessive puking, and among other things, the good ole toothbrush trick.

Come to find out, inside the FTC where they know everything like God knows everything, they told me I was a purging bulimic when I used laxatives.

Forced fecal ejection was their formal term. We called it 'puking out our ass' or 'shitting our brains out'. That was as fancy as we got with that 'number two' business.

After six months of puking more in a toilet than sitting to shit, I had pondered much on the similarities and differences of puke and feces.

People are more prone to vomit when they see a person vomiting versus someone taking a crap. We defecate all the time, everyday, sometimes more than once a day. We're used to it. Puking on the other hand is occasional, like when you're sick or you drank too much.

I was obsessed with the whole idea of binging and purging. I read about the Roman aristocrats and their fancy feasts in Dr. Shoerner's *Blood and Guts, Wine and Lust: Dining with a Roman Aristocrat.* These aristocrats were fed by slaves at a *triclinium.* This was three fainting couches joined around a table full of food and wine. They would engorge themselves then purge everything, binge and purge, again and again, all while getting drunk. It was my kind of party.

A slave was designated to clean up the vomit. The details of these dinner parties didn't bother me much, but it was Dr. Shoerner's suggestion that there may have been what is called *emetophilia,* or sexual arousal from puking, that made me gag and puke a little in my mouth.

Dr. Shoerner also suggested that some Romans may have used a *spongia* as an emetic (or puking device) which was a communal sea sponge on a stick that Roman's would use to wipe there ass with, of course rinsing it afterward. So if a Roman wanted to puke at the toilet instead of at the table, he would just go grab a *spongia* and get on with his emesis.

I had gotten so accustomed to vomit and vomiting that only those two things, the *spongia* or *emetophilia,* could make me ill. Everything else was fine.

Chapter 7: Fish

After I was done brushing my teeth, I went and met my roommate, Allen. I asked him if he would tattle about the puking.

He shook his head "no".

Allen was a quiet and awkward kid, and during his first week in the FTC witnessed a kid hanging dead from a pipe. This didn't help his quietness and awkwardness. He had a roly-poly physique and was nice as pie. I guessed he would wrestle at 172 lbs. He was diagnosed with Major Depressive Disorder and prescribed Freshax. Freshax was the go-to drug for everyone's problems, and a huge money maker for FTC and the Santomon pharmaceutical company, Proxy and Keno, which created it. I would have been prescribed Freshax if it wasn't for Dr. Pavlovich and my Histrionic Personality Disorder.

In the FTC, these psychological classifications and prescriptions became as important as being a human. It was your name tag. "What are you in for?", is what inmates in jail ask each other. The FTC patients ask "What's your disorder?" or "What are you on?".

In wrestling, Allen would be classified what wrestlers call a Fish. Real fish flop around when pulled out of water. Wrestler Fish flop around the same way, trying not to get pinned. I was a Fish when I started wrestling, so I knew firsthand the feelings of being tossed around, or how it was to wiggle and squirm for survival. I experienced the pain and humiliation of being put into the uncommon and difficult moves just to have your father watch when the referee slapped the mat. They give you an Honorable Mention ribbon, usually yellow, which was nothing more than a nice way of telling you, "Thanks for trying, come again". In wrestling, "Wimps need not apply", this is the shirt the dickhead wrestler that pinned you would wear. Sometimes, this survival of the fittest turns a Fish into a Shark, but that path is littered with physical and emotional hardships, trust me, I know.

This is why I always supported the Fish on my team. Regrettably, I was never too sympathetic with the ones I wrestled in matches.

Most Fish wrestle at the junior varsity level. If you happened to be one of those skilled underclassmen that couldn't beat the Senior at your weight class, you end up wrestling with at least one or two Fish.

Since boys will be boys, which means being cruel, your teammates might make a list of difficult moves for you to do. If you do all the moves in sequence before pinning the poor kid, they will buy you a can of chewing tobacco or porno mag or some other teenage prize.

The spectacle of a Fish flopping around is not much different than gladiators chasing down prisoners, the weak versus strong of violent entertainment. Your teammates always want to see the painful moves such as the *banana split* or the *squealer cradle* or *double chicken wing*, and meanwhile the poor Fish's father (or unlikely mother) is in the stands cringing at the sight. They pray for a quick pin like a sharp axe for beheading, mercy.

Sometimes they want you to do weird or rare moves like the *crucifix* which was my favorite. I'd be the crossbeam of the crucifix and my opponent would be Christ.

They love to see throws of *grand amplitude* which pays five points in freestyle and Greco-roman wrestling. This is when you hip toss the poor Fish in a drastic arc.

I tried to get a two-way conversation going with Allen. It didn't amount to much. I asked some questions and he grunted or grumbled or simply said ‘yes’ or ‘no’. I asked him what he was in for, not the standard questions I was suppose to ask, and he made a sentence. “Because my mom’s a bitch!”

This was how our conversations went for the first couple of days, with me rambling or ranting and Allen grumbling.

After telling me the story of the kid he saw swinging from the pipe with his blue tongue hanging out, he opened up to me.

We became friends.

Chapter 8: Solitaire

In most correctional facilities, the situations are similar. Whether you're in a *bone fide* sanitarium, a jail or prison so said my brother Cy, or in the well-to-do treatment center like the FTC, it's empty in the morning and crowded for the rest of the day after lunchtime. I learned in FTC to utilize that morning time for *alone time*. It's a nice time to play a game of solitaire or to write.

On that second day, I went to the dayroom looking for the new girl. All I found was a mouthful of kids with too many problems. In these types of facilities, nothing is specialized. For adults, you can go somewhere when you're too fat or too skinny, when you do too many drugs or drink too much, or when you're crazy. There's a place for every symptom.

In the FTC, the hyperphagics (overeaters) and bulimics and anorexics eat together. Their contrast is their conflict. When a hyperphagic or bulimic eats, it no longer represents civilized dining, we devour our meals like a monster consumes lambs. This is the last thing a person struggling with anorexia wants to see when they are attempting to eat.

I was often told by my mom to slow down and enjoy my food, easy for her to say. I could not slow down, though I did enjoy it. She also punished me when I chewed the *body* and gulped the *blood* of Christ during Eucharist. "You're supposed to hold it in your mouth until it melts away." She often admonished me whispering on the way back to the pews. My father mocked her once, he said at one of his rare appearances at church, "you shouldn't rush when you're eating God." Coming from my dad, I knew what he meant because he had a great respect for rituals, but this was a definite slight towards mom. My mother told him to leave mass.

The only difference in treatment is the group that they get put into. Someone was wise enough to separate the *lardasses* from the *skeletons*, because you can't tell a hyperphagic to eat less as you tell an anorexic to eat more.

The dayroom at the FTC provided a prime example as to why the opposite sides of eating disorders shouldn't be confined together.

Too many times I heard an outburst like "fatty" or "eat something".

As a teenager entering the FTC, imagine getting thrown together in a McMill's cattle yard grazing, doped and crazed. Everyone spreading their own particular type of disease to the rest of the herd then you go to slaughter and get ground up and fried on a McMill's grill and thrown onto a bun made from Santomon's franken-flour topped with lettuce and tomato poisoned with Santomon's pesticides, served on the plate of glutton America. You are what you eat, a mephitic super-burger.

If prison was a school for criminals like Cy often said, treatment centers were schools for psychological disorders and addictions. Polish your trade. Get an edge on Life.

You could find Jenny the Cutter, Johnny the Animal Abuser, or me-Jake the Upchucker. Everybody had a history and a trick. And if you'd like to learn, someone was there to teach you. Cy said the same goes in prison. Some steal and some murder. In a treatment center, some hurt themselves for attention and some hurt something else for attention, some get addicted to attention. Where ever you found yourself, someone would teach you whatever it was you wanted to know. Puking was my talent, but everyone either already knew how or didn't care.

I wasn't concerned with other people's baggage. I didn't give a shit how or why Jenny cut little slashes into her arm with a box-knife. But she told me anyway, they always told me anyway. I told her to use a gun next time and that would solve the problem. I didn't talk to Jenny after that. People don't want real solutions, they want attention. And at the FTC, they get it.

Without me caring, Johnny told me how and why he tortured dogs and cats. I asked him when he was ready to move on to humans. A creepy little smile for a response and I didn't have to talk to him anymore. I crossed my fingers for hookers worldwide.

Freddy told me about how he could drink six *forty ouncers* of St. Agni's Premium Malt Liquor. I told him he shouldn't waste his time with beer and that he should stick to vodka or better yet, if he wanted to destroy his liver he should quit eating and drinking water and find some moonshine. That'll do the trick.

I waited in the dayroom for the new girl only to hear a handful of petty problems. Everybody had something wrong with them. Besides my bulimia and alcoholism and anger, my real problem was that I had refused to accept that I had any problems whatsoever.

I was my father's son, an angry alcoholic eschatologist waiting for the world to end.

The FTC is the place you're sent to if you talked back to your parents or if you tried to slice your wrists the wrong way, crossing the railroad tracks instead of following them. It's a new set of parents for the parents who broke you and couldn't fix you.

When Allen and I got to be on the conversation level, he confided in me his situation. We were half-wrestling in the space between our beds, I was showing him how to *lock up* and the *single leg takedown.*

"Jacob." Allen said. We stood there catching our breath. "You want to know why my mom put me in here."

I nodded.

"Because I stayed in my room too much. I liked to read my comic books and fantasy books and I like to write stories. She found one of my stories. It was about a knight that turned and plunged his sword into his own belly after waiting centuries for his lover. She was captured by a dragon and freed by another knight who ended up marrying her. It was just a silly fantasy story, but she thought I was depressed. She thought that 'people don't like me' and that 'I have no friends' let alone a girlfriend. She went on for hours about me and my depression. She cried and kept saying sorry that she messed up as a mom. She wouldn't listen to me, I told her that I was okay with not being social and that I don't feel sad all the time like she thought. I felt fine before I got here, far better than how these zombie pills make me feel now." He said.

"She should be the one locked up, crazy moms. My situation was kind of the same. I don't think I have a problem with bulimia or my drinking and so what if I get angry now and then, who doesn't? But apparently I'm 'too out of control' for my mom to handle. To be honest with you Allen, I don't think there is anything wrong with any of us. It's the society that wrong, this place is wrong. Who are they to tell us how to feel, what to think? They just want our parent's money, and they want to train us for prison." I said.

I was comforted to hear Allen speak so confidently. He was starting to trust me.

Chapter 9: Group in the Toilet

In the FTC, there were designated counseling groups that you were put in which target your individual problems. Everyone called it 'group', much like how you use 'dinner', as in "I have to go to Group." According to my problems, I had Anger Group on Monday and Friday, Eating Disorder Group (or ED Group) on Tuesday and Thursday, and Addict Group on Wednesday. I met Ana in my first Ed Group on a Tuesday.

All of my problems were interwoven into my Groups. In Anger Group, there was a childish illustration of my addiction and disorders and negative emotions as my naughty friends huddled around me making me behave badly.

In most Groups, they sat you in small classroom in circular fashion, for equality, or probably some corporate asshole's fantastic vision of King Arthur's roundtable and whatnot.

If there was anyone new to the group they did introductions. And there was always fresh meat, so you had to explain again and again why you don't eat or why you eat everything you see just to throw it all back up. You had to explain why you liked to stick needles in your arm or drink to blackout. The new kid had to listen to how your uncle touched you and how you felt empty inside.

The FTC put kids who suffered from *hyperphagia*, the overeaters, in their own ED Group. But the two groups would never cease to internally fight an epic war of eating disorder slurs like *beanpole* or *lard-ass*. But due to the restrictions of a monitored environment such as the FTC, you would hear code words like *bully* or *annie* from the obese camp and *rolly* or *tarp* from the jejune camp. I learned that *tarp* was invented by some clever anorexic girl to portray what an obese person's clothes were crafted from. The list of slurs goes on and on.

The counselor always started, same way every time. They would start with a rehearsed sketch of who they are and some of the stupid things they like, and maybe some silly hardship they experienced. In my first ED Group, there were two counselors, the leader and another sitting next to the new girl. Both counselors were young women. There were always women counselors in the ED Group. The lead counselor gave us her recital, half-true and barely there. She looked at each girl in the circle all the while, but I never saw her glance at me. She wouldn't acknowledge me. I assumed she had daddy-issues. At the FTC, we are all pretend psychologists.

The introductions went around quickly during my first Group. I knew it was awkward for a male to be in such a group, and it showed, we were all uncomfortable. The girls didn't want to vomit all their problems into this toilet-shaped group when a male was intruding. Even I was toilet-shy.

"My name is Jacob McAlister. I like to cook and I like to eat, but I need to make weight for wrestling. So I usually puke in the toilet when I'm finished eating. Not a big deal really." I said.

I wanted to say "I don't care if I look fat or not" or "I don't care if anyone thinks I'm attractive", but after hearing the girls before me complain of nothing but fatness and insecurity, I figured I shouldn't. I estimated the weight of the entire room of thirteen people to be under the average weight of a heifer cow, since 'heifer' was the choice word for four of the girls to describe themselves. I truly felt bad for them and really felt like I was intruding.

Much like the introductions before me, the rest complained of looking in the mirror and feeling ashamed of being fat and unattractive, until it was *her* turn, the new girl who was force-fed at my table.

I was intent on the new girl speaking, but the second counselor was there to read her written testimony. She was a voluntary mute.

My name is Ana. I'm seventeen. I'm diagnosed with the following, Anorexia Nervosa and Bi-polar Personality Disorder. I'm not anorexic because I think I look obscenely obese. I think that everyone is a gluttonous slob who...

The counselor stopped at that and mumbled in Ana's ear. Ana motioned at her with her finger for the woman to keep reading.

...who can't get enough...who can't buy enough...who can't devour enough. So that leads to my second diagnosis. I love all these beautiful creatures and plants and things. This makes me ecstatic, but to see these things murdered and destroyed for nothing but an insatiable urge or an irrational vanity, well this...makes me brutally angry. So yes, I got over the fact that my stepdad tried to molest me. And yes, I got over the fact that I'll never be the most beautiful or perfect. But I will not get over the people who only see themselves. I do not want to be one of these unconscious devourers of everything. Sickly human omnivores.

My fists were balled up. Something in the mention of Ana getting molested caused a visceral reaction, my guts were tight and buzzing. Rape and molestation stories were more common in the Anger Group, and regardless of what anybody thinks about a person, a girl talking about themselves getting raped will always make someone feel enraged.

I thought it peculiar to be called Ana the Anorexic, but Ana wasn't her real name. I had never heard of the Pro-Ana movement that supported anorexia as a lifestyle choice and not a disease. She was and always will be Ana to me. She hated her birth name and refused to acknowledge it. Everyone in the FTC addressed her as Ana.

The basic concept of Pro-Ana, the treatment of anorexia as lifestyle choice and not a disease, was fine with her. But what she wasn't okay with was with the reasoning behind the lifestyle, she had lived that way herself and had recently denounced the movement as vain. "Until the cause is selfless and not selfish, I want no part of it." She told me. She thought most anorexic girls were anorexic because of vanity, disorder or not. She told me that some such girls worshipped an Ana figure as a goddess of beauty to which they could devote themselves to, for themselves. She loathed this way of selfish thinking. But she did keep with her the ideal cosmic woman of Ana as her personal goddess. She was dead set on setting an example of how to starve oneself for a political and spiritual cause rather than waste away in one's own self-worship and self-loathing.

Ana would come tell me why she became a voluntary mute. Since she had been placed in these treatment facilities since she was twelve, her voice had gotten her into worse situations than the original one she had been set into. As a mute of any sort, you get special treatment. Or you get left alone most of the time. In addition, she was practicing non-violence.

Her mantra for language was: *The voice of a human is violent even when it's peaceful.*

My attraction to Ana besides her pure beauty, on all levels, was her devotion, she had a purpose beyond herself. Although I didn't understand it at the time, I grew to appreciate and emulate it. She had very powerful ideas and meant them from the bottom of her huge heart.

Ana thought that most of these girls should just slice their wrists or take one too many pills and just end it as some do, if they're not committed to doing something other than wallow in self-pity, why live? Her main objection was the amount of selfishness involved in the whole concept of eating disorders. She felt that starving yourself should have a purpose beyond one's self. This she likened to Gandhi, or other hunger-strikers. She taught me about the political prisoners of the IRA and about the Tamil revolutionaries. Ana was a wellspring of knowledge, an omnivorous reader, though she preferred to call herself a *frugivorous* reader.

After Ana's counselor read her introduction. I felt at ease staring at her. Everyone else was. She had a calm face and looked somewhere on the floor. She looked up at me for a half-second, my belly fluttered.

So at my next opportunity, I set out after Ana. I was more persistent and aggressive than I had ever been with a girl, before and after.

Chapter 10: Pro-Ana

Ana had said to me that I was 'awkwardly aggressive'. She was intrigued by me, and I didn't know why.

After that first ED Group, I spent anxious hours in the day room. Ana read the Bible in her room. She always read, whenever there was idle time. She wasn't Christian but reading was eating for Ana and even the Bible was better than listening to everyone's selfish problems.

She said she was closest to being a Jain more than anything. Jainism, one of the oldest living religions in the world, exists in India. Its followers practiced *fructarianism* by only eating fallen fruit and non-violence.

Jains believe in an endless cycle of evolution and devolution. The cycle starts with eight mile tall giants sustaining off of perfect fruits, world peace. It ends with three foot creatures, cave dwelling and violent as ever. We humans are to devolve into such creatures (not far off at the rate we're going). Out of the mixture of her own personal values and that of Jainism, Buddhism, Hinduism, and Taoism, she made her own religion called Ana-ism.

After the lag time of us *meal cautions*, I cut her off on the way to the female wing. I told her to come meet me in the day room after Shift Change. She raised her eyebrows and went to her room.

"I was in your group today…" I stopped when she turned into her room.

I went back to my room and pouted with Allen. He always looked like he was pouting, he wasn't. He blamed that on the medication.

I was restless and nervous and paced around our room.

The nurses changed shifts and checked the patients twice a day each. According to my brother, the guards in jail or prison did the same thing. In adult correctional facilities, they called it *count time*. In the FTC, they called it “Alone Time for Self-Reflection”. Patients called it ‘Shift Change’. The FTC didn’t want you to think or feel that the patients should be counted like sheep, though that was how we were treated. The FTC knew that counting would imply that someone might escape, they didn’t want you to think about that. They just wanted to make you “better” and “happy”. Yet the nurses counted each patient at the change of a shift to make sure a sheep hadn’t wandered off the pleasant pasture.

Although I figured Ana wouldn’t be out to meet me, there I was playing solitaire, flouncing with my feet.

Occasionally throughout the day, a different nurse came with medications or so-called vitamins for me and the two other Histrionic Disorders.

Ana was bi-polar so she had to come get her dosages of Freshax. Freshax became the household name for all anti-psychotic or anti-depressant medications, much like saying Jello for gelatin. Ana would tell me that most of these drugs were as helpful as a bullet in the head. Just another scam from the flimflam man.

The first couple of times I approached Ana, I was timid and nervous. She ignored me and walked to her room. Then I decided to write her a note.

It read:

I want to get to know you. I’ll be in the day room.

I was standing at the back of the line when the last round of meds was called. I already took my multi-vitamin, but I needed a way to cut off Ana long enough to make her take the note. The medication nurse was being overly cautious with her about hiding her pill underneath her tongue. I wasn't nervous anymore, actually kind of irritated.

I blocked her way when she was approaching. I thought she might try to barrel right through me, but she stopped right in front of me, strangely close. She looked me right in the face and lifted her eyebrows and shoulders - *What?*

"Here." I said. She was a head shorter than me, and since she was so close to me I didn't want to jam the note in her face. So I slipped it down to her hand. She took it.

This was one of those clear moments that lovers never forget. Neither person knows what the other is feeling at the time. It is this emotionally charged moment where everything ceases to exist aside from the lovers themselves, only their eyes and hands, hearts and writhing viscera remain.

She went to walk through me, I moved aside. I felt famished, in my stomach and in my heart. That one second of time and that faint touch of her hand when she grabbed the note left me without my body's unconscious ability to breath.

My face was flush.

I went back to solitaire, pretending to play. My head was jumping everywhere. I kept repeating to myself that she wasn't going to come out and that she wasn't interested in the likes of me. I kept looking at the clock.

It was five minutes before shift change and bedtime. Ana came to my table and sat sideways on the chair.

Chapter 11: Taste-test

I was staring at Ana while she stared off at everything but me and the TV. This went on for days.

"There's only five minutes left." I said.

She shrugged then wrote in her notebook and handed it to me.

I'm here, aren't I?

I caught her looking at me while I was reading. I handed the notebook back.

"You are." I said.

You're awfully aggressive. What's your intention?

"I haven't thought of it. I just like you."

You must want something from me. You're a boy. You're not going to get in my pants if that's what you're thinking.

"I wasn't thinking of that, honestly. You're pretty and you seem interesting. I want to get to know you."

Sure you do. You want to get to know me enough to have sex with me so you can tell all your friends that you screwed an anorexic chick.

"Not at all. If you don't believe me, you can go about your day. I'll leave you alone."

We sat there, neither of us looking at each other. Ana started writing again.

Well, you're not very romantic are you?

"No I'm not. Sorry."

Don't apologize. I wouldn't still be sitting here if you were. Your lack of tact and your impatience makes me want to believe you. Until tomorrow.

Ana got up and walked away. She was testing me and I didn't care. I was possessed.

That night I rolled around in bed thinking about our interaction. I convinced myself that her meeting me was a gesture of interest. That thought was enough to help me to sleep.

I had to constantly remind myself that I had to earn her trust. I was a male in a world where men have a horrible history of imposing their will on to females. Why would I be any different than any other guy that had come on to her?

But I came to her with no apparent walls, and this both intrigued and bothered her. During my clumsy courtship she wrote me. *You haven't had your heart truly broken yet.* She was right. I had no defense against loving someone who could ultimately crush my heart. This fact led her to think twice about me.

Ana had little trouble seeing the truth in my actions. She knew I was sincere. But she had a long list of issues with love and with men which was why she had built an impregnable fortress guarding her emotions. She was so reluctant to let me in, and this was due to my sincerity and persistence. Ironically, my persistence, which she despised at first, ended up uniting us as lovers.

There were a handful of times during that fragile period of us getting acquainted that she would reach out in subtle ways, a touch on the leg or a vague written compliment to show interest. She wanted me to know not to give up on her.

She explained to me later that much of her demeanor was to test me. And when she felt comfortable she wrote, *I was far too interested in you to let you know it. I was afraid of how I felt.*

We started off simple and slow. All we had was time. I didn't realize this until after a week of being locked-up in the FTC. I started off counting the minutes, but after a week I didn't pay attention to the time or date. I was only concerned with Ana when I wasn't in my room with Allen or at my sessions with Dr. Pavlovich.

Ana and I spent all of our day room and recreation time together, getting to know each other, exchanging all those little trite things like our favorite things. Occasionally we'd share some deeper stuff like our personal histories. But I learned very little about Ana's deeper self until after getting out of the FTC. Her steadfast voluntary muteness had gotten in the way of her ability to express herself at hand and she didn't want to write an autobiography for me. *Much of my past should never be recorded,* she once wrote. She would apologize later for this very thing, though I didn't figure it an issue, I loved her, pure and simple. And I was ignorant to how much depth she possessed, I could only see what I was able to. The partial story of her life that she gave me in the FTC was far deeper than I had ever seen. And I thought I had some friends with tragedies in their lives, her past made their hardships look like a cakewalk.

Ana's voluntary muteness and her little notebook were a blessing to our acquaintance. I was bulimic and an omnivore. To her, I was both of these things purely out of selfishness. Ana despised both bulimia and excessive consumption, and her little notebook had held her back enough for us to not get into debates, or better yet a full blown argument. She let me slide on many things that she despised in the beginning. Others were not so fortunate. She hated most people. She wouldn't use the word *hate* though, hatred implied violence and Ana was in the ever-going process of rejecting violence. She preferred to use the word 'dismiss'. She 'dismissed' all those who were actively destroying the planet without regard.

In the FTC, it was not uncommon for kids to *hate* or *dismiss* all of the people surrounding them. But with Ana, her disdain was rooted with very complex justifications, not just the run-of-the-mill teenage angst.

In Group, she had been able to convey some of these things to others.

Julia was one of three models in our Ed Group, out of ten of us. She was known for spewing emotions and had the typical list of anorexic characteristics - sexual abuse, father abandonment, mother detachment, delusional self-perception, the whole smorgasbord. She was finally opening up one day with this long cathartic confession of her problems. She was crying and telling everyone all these bottled-up thoughts and feelings, only to have Ana pass her a note which ended everything.

Julia went back to her old shut-down self, just like before. I asked Ana about what she wrote afterwards. She wrote a cryptic tidbit.

If no one loves you, and you don't love yourself, what's the point? You know there are easy ways to end all this. Enough with the charade.

She knew better than to let one of the counselors read it, and she wrote to me, *it wouldn't have had the same effect if a counselor read it aloud.*

The other girls would get a random retort that Ana managed to get the counselors to read, but I never got the pleasure of getting criticized by Ana until we left FTC. I didn't set myself up either. My contributions to the Group Toilet were everything but self-loathsome and emotional. I kept a steady flow of little facts about puking and wrestling and food, my three fascinations.

In regards to bulimia, I had told my Group that the Romans loved to vomit, as much as they loved to eat, that didn't go over well. I let everyone know that I felt like a Roman when I puked and a Greek when I wrestled and both when I cooked. I had gotten nothing but dumb looks except from Ana, who watched me with a gentle and observant face.

I told them that Seneca said it best. """*Edunt ut vomant, vomunt ut edant.* They eat to vomit, they vomit to eat." I had memorized the Latin to make myself sound smart. I was showing off for Ana, she wasn't impressed. I told them about Roman vomit-inducing feathers and how I planned to use one. The girls and the counselors were uninterested. I didn't care.

Every time I read something new about puking, I would share it with Group. For example: when I read about Kronos eating his children except for Zeus, who was replaced by a rock which was puked out and became the navel of the universe. The ED counselors had a problem with me talking about vomit-type-things so freely, they thought I was promoting bulimia. I told them I wasn't, that it was my way of dealing with my eating disorder. They believed me.

In Emotion Group, I explained how Hercules murdered his whole family in an unprovoked maniacal rage. Now that's anger. The Emotion Group counselors removed me from the Group in certain instances, they did not tolerate my promotion of anger and violence. They didn't believe me when I told them that it was part of my own treatment.

In Substance Abuse Group, I got the same treatment from those counselors as I did with the Emotion counselors. They did not like the stories about the Greeks and Romans with their binge drinking and eating at the parties for their Gods. With any reference to the dancing and singing gods, Dionysus or Bacchus, they threatened immediate ejection.

I can't say I didn't walk away with anything from the Groups, but this is no comparison to how much two people affected me. Ana was the most important person, my love and spirit. But I also left the FTC with a great friend and mentor, Dr. Pavlovich.

Chapter 12: Shrink

My visits with Dr. Pavlovich didn't feel like 'therapy'. As I said before, I didn't realize until later that he was actually treating me. He developed his own method of counseling called the Tribal Method which consisted of spending many hours with patients in their natural environment, as a friend or mentor.

This method didn't have much success in the psychology world. Dr. Pavlovich himself would go on to say in an interview in *Psychology Now*: "It's not that this method is unpopular because it's ineffective, but it is very inefficient, as in, not cost-effective. And it is very difficult to execute when a counselor doesn't truly care about his or her patient. Of course there are exceptions, but in this method, patients aren't paychecks."

During the interview, he always resorted to standard treatment procedures if he felt any negativity towards a patient during the first visit. He said that a psychologist would have to have the peaceful and loving demeanor of a Buddhist monk in order to respect everyone. He admitted that he was far from being a monk, and that most psychologists are liars if they think they care about all of their patients. "Most want money, and they lie when they say that they really care."

He told me in our last session, "If everyone is full of shit, including yourself, things will run smoothly. But when you seek truth, you expose everyone's lie, and for this they will hang you." He gave common examples like Jesus and Copernicus. He also said there was a more eloquent version of this idea written by Thoreau.

Dr. Pavlovich talked to me mostly about my interests. On some days we'd chat, on others he let me read something interesting out of his small library while he worked on whatever it was he had to.

Over time, I spilled my guts.

From the start, he showed interest in what I liked or what I thought. He also shared many of the same interests, and he was honest with his interest in these things. If the man was anything, he was honest, maybe too honest for most.

"Tell me about wrestling." Dr. Pavlovich said, in front of his wall 'o' books.

"How do you know I'm a wrestler? Is it in my charts?" I said.

"No, it's not in your charts, just a good guess. I figured you weren't a jockey, judging by your stature, though I shouldn't assume. There have been jockeys your size. I didn't want to make the assumption that you're a ballet dancer, that might offend you. And…I've never met a bulimic boxer yet." He said.

"I've been wrestling since I was a child. My dad wanted my brother and I to be able to defend ourselves. He also taught us boxing at home."

"Are you bulimic? They put that in your charts, but I want to know what you say." He said and went to his coffee station. "Coffee?" He pointed a mug at me.

"Yes sir. I'll take it black."

He handed me the coffee and reclined. "We're not in the army, you don't have to call me 'sir'."

"Sorry." I said.

"Don't apologize."

"You're here because of your Histrionic Personality Disorder, not bulimia. It doesn't really matter much to me though. You're forced to spend time here with me, and they pay me to pretend to fix you. But I'm not going to pretend to fix you. If you think you have a problem that needs work, I help you. Otherwise, it's up to you on what you want to do with our time. Read, write, talk, whatever you want. I'm just happy I could save you from their pills." He said.

Dr. Pavlovich was like one of those uncles who actually gave a damn about what you were doing with your life. He always asked what I thought about this thing or that. Going to his office wasn't like going to Group or some other function made to repair your faults. It was a place to go in the FTC where you did not have to worry about anything. This in itself was therapeutic.

"Have you wrestled Greco-Roman style?" Dr. Pavlovich said.

"Not yet, only folk-style and freestyle. I've messed around during practice, so I know the rules." I said.

Both Folk-style and Freestyle wrestling had evolved from a British form of wrestling called Catch wrestling or catch-as-you-can wrestling. This form spread through the craze of the carnival in the 19th century. Carnival wrestlers would combat the tough-guys of local populations without the rules of the Greeks and the Romans. In Greco-Roman style, you're limited to maneuvers above the waist.

We talked about wrestling and other ancient sports, mostly ones in the original Olympics. I learned more about the Greeks and the Romans. Dr. Pavlovich taught me about *pankration* (or *pankratos)* which was the original form of mixed martial arts, literally meaning 'all strengths'. This combined wrestling with boxing and became the ultimate sport for the ancient Greeks.

He told me that the ancient Greeks embraced violence in their culture as an important factor to the human existence, but the Romans had exalted it for cultural domination and mimicry.

"Have you wrestled before?" I asked.

"Never have. But I've always been fascinated by it. I believe it to be the genesis of sport. The ancient *homo sapiens* must have wrestled for sport. " Dr. Pavlovich said.

In many conversations we had, he used the words 'ancient' and 'primal' and 'tribal'.

"I was in track and field as a teenager. My dad was a marathon runner. I wasn't athletic as a kid though, and I hated running. I did take a liking to shot-put, discus, and javelin though. I was never really good in high school, but my persistence paid off in college." He said.

He dug into his desk and handed me a pewter medal. It was gun-metal gray and had Honorable Mention written diagonally under a silhouette of a discus athlete, poorly embossed.

"I got this during my first season in high school. I always kept it as a reminder of how failure can bring strength."

I knew it all-too-well. This was the fourth place, the made-up place of recognition. It was created to keep kids from crying at the end of a competition. It didn't work for me and for most others, I cried all the time in the beginning.

In the Olympics, there are three medals. When you're a kid, sometimes there is this extra medal or ribbon to make a kid who lost think that he did okay, regardless that he didn't win at all. You can't fool children that easily, they know what's going on, they keep score. It was a reminder throughout a poor kid's life that they 'tried' once-upon-a-time, whether they ended up quitting or not.

These fourth place ribbons or medals were always given in round-robin Freestyle wrestling tournaments where four guys get put in a group and all have to wrestle each other.

I *won* so many of these prizes. I was the frumpy little fish flopping around the mat every tournament. Quite often, I was the practice dummy being manhandled while my father screamed, "get him!" Although I was in no position to get anyone, I just kept squirming to keep my shoulder off the mat.

I handed it back to him and nodded.

"I knew you would appreciate the symbolism." He said.

"Yeah, I've got a whole stack of these. I was a *fish* when I was younger. Fish is what we call weak wrestlers. It's kind of mean, but then again so is giving them *pink belly*." I said.

"I never forget those failures. I've seen too many people throw their talents to the wind, because they weren't interested in what they were good at. The gifted take their talent for granted. I've also seen many people give up, because they weren't instantly good at something. But you have the passion which comes from persistence. You're impassioned by the sport." He said.

"I love it when the season ends. I don't enjoy all the practice and matches and weight-watching. It's nerve-racking. But I spend the rest of the year thinking about how great it is." I said.

"It's great how that works, how all the hardships that the mind and body endeavor create euphoric memories. I find this with all things in life. We don't need the scientific proof to know some of these human concepts." He said.

Dr. Pavlovich introduced me to many ideas, mainly within philosophy and mythology and psychology, things I was most interested in.

We also talked about Ana and her greatness.

Chapter 13: (Rule #4: No Touching/Heavy Petting)

Rule #4 – No Touching. The FTC prohibited the embodiment of all things physical, violent and sexual. Rule #4 was concise and vague and by far the most disregarded rule on the list. The laminated signs will be forever graffitied by changing the first letter in *Touching*. With a pen stroke, someone prohibited the patients from Douching, then Pouching, and with a few more strokes, the mysterious act of Foucking.

The censoring and euphemizing by the FTC creators was so extreme yet the only real book that you were allowed to read was the Bible, the great book of sex and war. I had checked to see if they had censored the Bible, they hadn't.

My half-Jewish friend David thought that the leaders of cults, religions et cetera, must never think that the average person can get through all of the Jewish genealogy to get to the meat of some stories, especially the graphic ones. Often, David tried to get me to read stuff in the Bible, but it was for different reasons than my mother forcing it on me. He felt that the handful of books that dominate the world, should be read and understood by everyone, then maybe all the nonsense might end.

I read the story of Sodom and Gomorrah, complete with the seduction of Lot by his daughters. Someone had graffitied the margins with their understanding of how Lot started his new tribes. Here was a clever little drawing made completely of sticks and circles - a man drinking a bottle of XXX with an enormous phallus that was held off the ground by two women who were each composed of three equal sized circles and five sticks. Apparently Lot was happy with incest according to the artist's depiction. I was tempted to sketch below that, Lot licking his pillar-of-salt wife, but I couldn't bring myself to do it. This was my mom's sacred book. People would have been executed for such things in the past.

I read the story of Joshua and Jericho, my friend David's favorite. On more than one occasion he made me read the lines in Genesis 6:20-21. I was tempted to underline and litter the margins with arrows to draw attention to the extent that God's people will go to heed His name. But again, I thought of my mom and also of Father O'Leary. And I knew that David would frown upon it though he had stopped practicing Judaism.

And they utterly destroyed all that was in the city, both man and woman, both young and old, and ox, and sheep, and ass, with the edge of the sword.

"The most sacred and famous self-help books have stories of genocide in them. You should learn Hebrew just to read this sentence." David once told me .

Besides reading violent and sexual stuff in the Bible, I read stuff that David had told me about my name. Parts he told me to read that I never did. Most times, David called me by the Hebrew pronunciation, *Yakov, w*hich he said loosely translates into 'leg-puller'. This amused me because I didn't care for leg takedowns.

In folk-style wrestling, single and double leg takedowns are staple moves. I should have been a Greco-Roman wrestler considering this.

I did some more vanity research which led me to read everything about Jacob. David always told me to read that section, but I always sloughed it off.

The biblical Jacob and I have a few things in common, wrestling and food.

In the Old Testament, Jacob bought his twin brother Esau's birthright with a bowl of stew (I love my mom's stew!). Jacob had dressed in goatskins to mimic his apish brother to trick his blind father Isaac into blessing him. They ate food and drank wine, dew from the heavens and fatness from the earth (I love food and wine). His dad couldn't take it back, Jacob had smelled of *Gan Eden,* in Hebrew - the Garden of God. The smell of Paradise.

Though I never had to compete with my brother for a blessing from my father nor did I climb a ladder to heaven to envision the Hebrew enemies.

I did wrestle with God, or my own version, *myself.* Biblical Jacob's other name is Israel, he who wrestles God. The angel or avatar of God touched Jacob's inner thigh. Along with other Hebrew traditions, David doesn't eat the last half of animals because of this.

And I do eternally smell of Paradise, or what I call Ana. But her version of Paradise was quite different, she thought it was a planet without humans, including herself.

***

Ana knew when and where we were able to touch each other. I was awkward at first, I didn't want her thinking that only wanted sex. Also, I was afraid of getting caught, I kept looking over her shoulder and mine during that first time. I was only daring and aggressive with Ana when I was trying to meet her. She initiated everything sexual between us, although she wasn't aggressive about it. I always followed her signal though she was passive and gentle. She never liked aggression during sex. She would stop me if I got too aggressive.

I was aware of the rules and not aware of what we could get away with. Ana knew where and when we could get away with things, not that consequences mattered to her anyway. She had had several boyfriends when locked up in treatment facilities. She was wise not to tell me until we were out of FTC, because when she did, I had a small bout of jealous rage.

Every person wants to think that they are the first and only one, the special and unique one, especially when it comes to teenagers. It takes years and so-called wisdom to realize that it doesn't matter about a significant other's sexual history, unless of course he or she was a prostitute. If a person's past doesn't follow them, they should be forgiven for being human.

Ana was a remarkable lover, always slow and passionate, she would have it no other way. I honestly figured that she just knew exactly what to do with no prior experience. I made myself believe that she was a virgin and was naturally good at fellatio and hand-jobs. I never questioned it at the time. This was all make-believe. Naivety is make-believing.

Because of Ana's lack of speech in the FTC, I filled in the blanks about her that suited me best. This little reality I created would be torn to bits after we left the FTC.

To make a complete and normal human being, the FTC uses a pie diagram to show what you need in your life. To fulfill the Physical piece of the pie, counselors take you out for recreation or 'Rec'. This is the time to skip through the tulips or play basketball or sneak off for some heavy petting. Ana knew all the secret spots where we came to know each other intimately.

As with most teenagers engaged in sexual activities, we started with the kissing and dry-humping with some light-petting then on to the heavy-petting. Terms like 'petting' are taught to you in middle school. They also teach you that when someone pleasures someone else's genitals it is called masturbation, but no one calls it that. Masturbation is usually applied for the self.

Ana showed me how good she was at all these sexual things and I tried to do the same. On Friday and Saturday nights, we were allowed to stay up late and watch a movie with the lights dim. Only one counselor worked in the dorm on third shift. These counselors generally didn't care what went on so long as it wasn't too obvious, sometimes they slept. The few nurses on third shift were in their own offices, only for emergencies.

Before the opening credits started, Ana and I had a hand down each other's pants. Any of the other kids were either doing the same or ignoring the petting fest. Everyone had a mouse wiggling around in their pants.

I was reluctant to go further than heavy-petting until I knew it was safe, until I knew that a counselor wasn't going to come around the bush and see the teenage version of the beast-with-two-backs. To ensure this, I had a chat with Chuck.

"Charles, can I ask you for a favor?" I said.

"Sure, what is it?" Chuck said.

"Is it possible for you not to come check on me and Ana next time you monitor outdoor Rec?" I asked.

"Have I before?" He said.

"No, I suppose not. I just wanted to make sure. Thanks."

"Not a problem." He said. "So you really like this girl?"

"Yeah, why?" I said.

"A lot of counselors have trouble with her. She's been in here quite a few times." He said.

"I'm not a counselor." I said.

"So, she's not as crazy as they say she is?" He said.

"No, she's not. She's perfect. Who isn't crazy anyway?"

He started to ask me something else then caught himself. I knew it was going to be about how skinny she was. As informal as our patient-counselor relationship was, he knew there was a line he shouldn't cross. I thought Ana was beautiful, I didn't care if other people saw her as a beanpole.

Chuck came to find out that my older brother was Cyrus McAlister. Chuck and many other guys had a lot of respect for Cy, he was a man's man.

***

Like the first sip of fine liquor or bite of a gourmet dish, the first time having sex with my true love had captured my heart. It wasn't a bout of acrobatics, just one embracing the other, insanely blissful.

The rest of our sex in the FTC was softly carnal and spiritually daring. Ana made sex possible during movie time in the subtlest of ways. She wore a full length skirt with no underwear. Everyone figured that she was sitting on my lap. I was not on earth in those moments, I was in Paradise. I had the smell of *Gan Eden.*

As for the first time, we had sex the day after Chuck gave the go ahead. We made love on a bed of grass. It was more intimate and sweeter than I could only daydreamed, and we were so bold as to get fully undressed. Ana was so bold, I only followed her lead.

She had gained some weight. She was not the bag of bones that she had been. Her clothes had hidden much of her female figure. Her body was a slender white violin, supple breasts with nipples of perfect contrast. Her waist was narrow and her hips were broader than her clothes ever revealed.

She was covered in hand-poked tattoos. She had a primitive outline of St. Catherine of Sienna across her chest. On her back was the scale of the Egyptian underworld, weighing the feather of truth against a heart. She had several iconic images on her arms, representing her devotion to animals and plants and Earth.

We devoured each other in the good way, the way one devours a last meal. Lips and limbs and hands everywhere.

When Chuck blew the whistle to line up, we were just finishing getting dressed. Then I heard Ana's voice for the first time.

"Do you love me?" She whispered in my ear.

I paused in shock, my hair raised.

"Yes… of course." I said.

That was it for the talking. She led me away by my hand, apparently giving up on rule #4 as we crossed the field to the line a kids ready to go back inside. I wanted to let her hand go so we wouldn't get in trouble, but the urge to be close to her was too great. It was the lovers' moment when neither one wants to let go, when neither one wants to give up first.

I looked at her eyes and the sky. The same blue, too vivid to be real.

Chapter 14: Arts and Crafts

To nurture your inner child and strengthen trust and self-confidence, the FTC had many different activities spread throughout the week. A frequent one was Arts and Crafts.

Ana and I were sitting together at a wooden table. She was making necklaces out of berrylike beads. Ana was lacing *cranberry* and *blueberry* beads. I was rolling out clay snakelike coils which get stacked atop each other to make a cup. This is the first piece of pottery you learn in school. My father considered this a survival skill.

The counselor told us to make something for one of our parents or influential relatives. I was making a cup for my mother, not to mend our relationship or show I cared, but as a smartass gesture of "thanks for locking me up Mom".

Something was wrong with Ana. I had sensed something was wrong immediately after we were done having sex during outdoor Rec.

I was watching her get dressed, adoring her, and looking at a tattoo on her belly of what looked like a spiral galaxy spinning around a pill shape. She had gained some more weight. It was a very little amount by *normal* standards. It was just enough for me to notice that her figure was filling out some in the places that women do.

She had been feeding herself at Meal Time with her head down and free hand blocking the view of her mouth.

During sex I had been more vigorous than before, aggressive enough for her to calm me down. I had thought this might have something to do with why she was upset. I didn't want to ask.

Then I stated the obvious. "You're upset." I was joining each coil, tail to mouth, and stacking them one slightly bigger than the one below.

She pulled out her notebook and wrote quickly. She shoved the notebook over by me.

I don't know what you think is going on here. I'm not your personal sex object. I know what you were thinking yesterday. You like the weight I've gained. But you better give up that idea. That's not who I am or what I'm about. I'm not one of those hussy girlfriends you're used to dating.

I read it a couple of times and sat there for awhile thinking of what to say. My first reaction was anger because she initiated all of our sexual activities. But I liked her so much, I had to think of something positive and reassuring.

"I just think you're beautiful, the same as the first day I saw you. I'm just trying to show it more and more when I can." I said.

I really wanted to tell her that she shouldn't treat *me* like a sexual object and that I wouldn't mind if she gained a few more pounds. But I knew if I said anything harsh, our zygote of a relationship would miscarry right then and there. Also, arguing out loud with a person who isn't speaking was awkward. I would have sounded like a nutcase if I raised my voice with insults. I felt some of that power that Ana had with being voluntarily mute. This was how she had some control over her counselors. I had seen it in their faces so many times already.

She wrote more:

I'm sorry, but I'm frustrated about a lot of things and it's so hard for me to communicate any of it. I have so much to ask about you. I know so very little. I feel I know you, but not very well. And you don't volunteer much. It'll be better when we can finally talk to each other. I don't know if you're playing coy for the sex or if you are sincere. I feel vulnerable with you.

"I'm not being coy. I'm vulnerable too." I said.

I grabbed the pen and notebook and wrote.

Why can't you just talk to me now?

She shook her head "no" and took her pad and pen back.

You're leaving soon.

She scribbled and then she went back to threading berries.

"Eventually. I don't know when though." I said.

Take me with you.

She wrote, flashed the notebook over and back then started writing again.

I'll be in here much longer than you. They're fed up with me. I'm an intolerable and incurable case to them. If the state wasn't paying for this treatment, they would commit me to the asylum. My last foster family has given up on me which I'm fine with. I have no one besides you. They're probably going to keep me here until I turn eighteen which is less than three months from now. I need you to help me. I won't be able to stand this if you go.

I told her I would help her but didn't know how. She reminded me of my privileges of knowing Cy's friend Chuck. *Maybe he could help us?* But before I talked to Chuck, I had to call my brother. It was a lot for me to ask of a guy I barely knew and who had only helped me so far because of my brother.

I told Ana that she was going to have to eat like she had been, not getting rid of it, and that she would need the strength to run as far as we would have to.

Chapter 15: One Point Escape

Cy finally came to visit.

I had plenty of time to think about busting Ana out. I figured that Cy would think the whole thing silly, which he did. And if he wouldn't help us, I had friends I could call to pick us up after the escape. I did need Cy to convince Charles to help us, and we needed a place to stay. There was no way I would've asked my mom.

My mom hated my bulimia and would have hated if I dragged home a politically motivated, anorexic, atheist girl who would no doubt share a bed with me. She was irate that I didn't call her while I was in there. This whole episode of her locking me up was somehow my fault. She had to waste all that money, lose all that sleep. She never admitted she was wrong, even years later.

Cy was a known tough-ass. He had done time in prison for a list of crimes he had committed when he was on crank, otherwise known as meth, or methamphetamines. He was built like a brick shithouse after that. He summed up prison as somewhere to read and lift weights and occasionally have a fight. Charles would no doubt listen to whatever he had to say.

"It's kind of like county jail without the uniforms." Cy had his fingers interlocked on the table. This was how he always looked when my dad and I would visit him in prison.

"And there are girls in here." I said.

"That's the only thing missing from prison." Cy said. "Sorry I hadn't visited sooner. I thought you'd be out right away. As soon as mom came to her senses, but apparently she has none."

"She blames this whole thing on me, just because she caught me drinking a few times, and she thinks I'm full blown bulimic." I was getting nervous while telling him about Ana. He had a large chip on his shoulder about women and would remain that way for some time.

"How's the food?" Cy didn't like to stay on topics that referred to anything emotional.

"It's gourmet. I was expecting garbage food."

"Sounds a bit like prison food. It was great and you got lots of it, but jail food's awful. You always feel hungry." He said.

We made small talk. Whenever he finished talking, he half-grinned and nodded, regardless of what was being talked about. A doctor could have just finished talking about how he was going to die of cancer in less than three months, and Cy would smile and nod.

"Dad's pissed that you're in here. He was thinking about coming back from Alaska to get you out, but I told him you wouldn't be in here long. Mom can't afford it." Cy said.

"He probably thinks I'm a sissy for the bulimia thing." I said.

"Yeah. That's the word he used." He said.

"So I have to ask you a question." I said.

"Let me guess, you want to come stay with me."

"Yeah." I couldn't look him in the face. "And my new girlfriend."

"No problem." Nodding and half-smiling then half-laughing. "You didn't get a girlfriend from here did you?"

"Actually yes."

"Hey little brother, girls are crazy enough as is. The one's in here must be extra blessed."

"It's not like that. Trust me."

"It's fine. Just giving you a hard time. There's only one way to learn anyway. And that's the hard way." He patted me on the shoulder. Cy was my father's son, he liked to drink beer along with whiskey and talk about surviving apocalypse.

"The only problem is that this girl, Ana, might not get released anytime soon, and I might be out of here next week. I need your help."

He agreed to help me, but he continued giving me a hard time all way until he left. He grabbed me up in a bear hug before leaving. He was so much bigger than me, definitely Super Heavyweight class.

***

In wrestling, there is a 'down' position and an 'up' position taken up by a bottom man and top man. Most kids make fun of this if they don't wrestle. Those same kids often make some sort of homosexual reference and look over their shoulder to see if a wrestler heard them. This position can start at the second or third round.

Being the bottom man can be awkward for a wrestler who just met a girl who decided to come see him in the singlet. As weird as puberty is on a kid, it gets weirder when your new girlfriend comes to see you in a singlet, wrestling's version of the leotard, only to have you pose on all fours with your pubescent bulge neatly presented to the audience.

The bottom man will seek either an 'escape' or 'reversal'. To escape, explosion is the key. A wrestler spends hours and hours of drills on escape moves. The two basic ones are the sit-out and the stand-up, and they are self-explanatory. These moves are broken up into sections and drilled excessively until one no longer needs to think about it.

***

I kept these moves in mind when I rehearsed the plot for Ana's escape. A few simple motions. Explosion. One point Escape.

Realistically speaking, the entire plan wasn't much of an escape. As much as the FTC was like jail or an asylum, it wasn't. It was much like a minimum security prison where inmates could walk away if they wanted. The only security measure FTC had were the staff and the automated clunky doors. The fence that surrounded the furthermost perimeter was there for show if anything.

But we were in the middle of Cornville, U.S.A., and Ana had entrusted me with her departure. So I took everything seriously.

***

Days before my release date and Ana's escape, I consistently checked on Ana's nourishment. I was concerned about her keeping her food down and being in good enough shape for the running she would have to do.

She wrote:

I haven't been able to keep it down as often as I should. I'm trying. I feel ill constantly.

I didn't give her a hard time about it. I reminded her of the distance we would have to cover.

Ana was no stranger to athleticism, I came to find out. Like me, she got her eating disorder through athletics. She was a ballerina for many years. I thought it was funny at first, Ana the Ballerina, but it made perfect sense. I could picture her, this beautiful petite dancer, spinning and leaping with grace. I was relieved to find it was real, I had hoped that she wasn't one of these girls obsessed with their image more than anything. I felt some satisfaction to know Ana had an eating disorder with what I used to call a *purpose*. She told me how she thought that athletic obsession was just as petty and obscure as models with image problems. Ana the Ballerina Shrink.

She showed concern though, about the eating and keeping the food down.

I feel sick most of the time.

***

At my last session with Dr. Pavlovich, I didn't spend a minute reading. I just wanted to talk to him, or hear him talk. I told him the plan, although he could have easily thwarted the entire thing. I trusted him.

In the spirit of escape, he reminded me the story of Icarus.

Icarus didn't listen to his father Daedalus. The handmade wing invention his dad made had two vulnerabilities. Daedalus told him not to fly too close to the sun else the wax on the wings would melt and not to fly too low to the ocean else the wings would dampen and fail. Icarus nearly burned from the sun and plummeted into the ocean and drowned.

"Much of the human psyche can be analogized by this myth, but I'll only mention one." He said. "Icarus, was given the harshest of lessons of moderation. Remember what your elders advise you to do, and don't be cocky. The Greeks have *Nothing too much* written on the Omphalos, or the navel of the universe. "

I wanted him to explain further, but that was his way. He told me to think about it and remember it.

He gave me his business card.

"Call me if you ever need to talk."

***

Escape day came, FTC served a fine breakfast, spinach soufflé and wedges of cantaloupe and toasted baguette spread with Neufchatel whipped with garlic and tarragon. The tarragon was a little much, but I still ate with delight.

Chuck wasn't talking at the breakfast table, he was casually glancing at the spectacle. All the eating disorders types eating at the same table. He was amusing himself with watching the hyperphagics literally make food disappear while their personal counselors tried to slow them down.

I was taking my time, bite by bite, counting my chews. I was trying to make Ana comfortable and relaxed about the way she was eating, at a snail's pace with her hand blocking her mouth.

She wasn't served the soufflé. The FTC had caved in to some of her demands. For eggs, she wrote, *No chicken fetuses*.

I watched her eat the baguette nibble by nibble like a mouse. Her baguette had cashew butter on it. She wasn't nervous - she loathed eating, and it couldn't get any worse for her than to eat in front of people. Especially, the hyperphagic kids. To them, she had her head turned. I would soon find out that that particular action, the indiscriminate shoveling of food into one's mouth, was the most disgusting to Ana. She despised that I did it.

Charles said only this to me. "When you get back to your room, strip your linens and pack up your things. You'll be released sometime after Rec."

He didn't want to be buddy-buddy with me. It wasn't like he was going to sneak in the prison key inside a birthday cake, but he was going to be at fault for his non-action. Weeks after, I found out that he got fired over our escape.

After all of us Meal Cautions were done with our digesting time, I headed for my room to talk to Allen.

Allen was in his bed reading when I got there. I had given him some of the books Dr. Pavlovich lent me. I kept the main book that interested me, *Dr. Mantha's Compendium of Myth and Legend*. I put it in my Survival rucksack with the rest of my stuff.

"Are you ready big guy?" I said.

"Yes, I am." He was confident and looked me in the face. This introverted, pudgy, 14-year-old was coming out of his shell. I would run into Allen years later, a completely different person. He would grow taller than me and be awkwardly skinny like a puppet with a big bobble-head. He'd become a big fan of hallucinogens.

I was too nervous to read or have an extensive conversation with Allen, so invited him out to the day room for a game of chess.

My mind was a toilet bowl maelstrom of chunky multicolored thoughts. I wanted so bad to be with Ana in a free environment, to be able to hold hands and kiss and hug without feeling like a thief. I wanted to be done with all of the pamphlets and worksheets about emotions and drugs and self-image.

I loathed almost everything about the place, the despotic nurses and condescending counselors, the clunky doors and over-dramatic procedures, the force-feeding of status quo values down unwilling teenage throats and the almost literal force-feeding of anorexics.

What I didn't hate, were the slim few people I met, such as Dr. Pavlovich and Allen and Charles, the wonderful gourmet food, and, of course, my sweet Ana.

Allen and I were playing chess and Ana came to watch. My eyes were constantly shifting from Ana to Allen to the pawns on the chessboard and to Charles standing by the nurse's station. The room was quieter than normal.

"Rec Time!" Charles said. We lined up in front of him. Standard procedure.

What I had Allen do was fake a seizure. This was completely unnecessary and over-the-top. If anything, it hurt the situation more than helped.

My idea was for Allen to create a diversion so Ana and I could get enough of a head-start that none of the nurses could catch us. I underestimated Ana's physical capacity in regards to running, but overestimated her knowledge of swimming.

***

The FTC's protocol on such a medical emergency was three steps.

First, do roll call and count.

Second, call for the nurse.

Third, tend to the patient. This was obviously inhumane and designed to prevent escapes, because escapees meant that the FTC would lose the money from the account for that patient, or the State for that matter.

In his termination meeting, Charles' defense was that he was saving someone from dying. The FTC told him. 'You clearly failed to follow protocol procedures. Pack your things. Good bye.' When I found out about it, I felt horrible. But Charles was glad to be rid of the place. He would have lost his job anyway when the government shut FTC down. Proxy and Keno, the titan of pharmaceuticals, fired all employees during the shutdown. In the following month, the facility was sold and reopened by a different pharmaceutical company under a different name.

He was one of the important people that testified against the FTC subsidy of the Proxy and Keno empire, its pharmaceutical owner. Many other lawsuits and crackdowns like this got swept under the rug.

The government pretended to intervene and break up these types of facilities. Human rights groups came to try and erase the concept of the *mass-produced* version of the treatment center, the McMill's of juvenile correction. In some facilities, disorders were no longer lumped together. Hyperphagics no longer sat next to the anorexics, let alone ate in the same room. The dirty street bandit with Attention Deficit Hyperactive Disorder (or ADHD) didn't share a room with the suicidal queen of the Goths who suffered from Severely Acute Depression (cute).

These treatment facility companies, subsidies of pharmaceutical corporations, were constantly changing names and deleting files. Chunks of their profits were dealt out to victims of that indiscriminate and flawed system.

The local news stations would expose the horrors and the tragedies that would happen in these facilities. Stories of kids getting bones broken or strapped to tables for 48 hours or longer would be broadcast for all to see. Kids could tell their parents "I told you so" or in my case "Thanks Mom".

Some kids would never forgive their parents for locking them up for mental problems that they, the parents and their flawed parenting, would ultimately be to blame. A little saying I heard several times in FTC was "Fucked up kids, fucked up parents." How's that for psychology?

***

Meanwhile, as Allen was frothing at the mouth and convulsing like a fish, Ana and I were sprinting towards the edge of a copse of trees where the FTC had a bordering fence, six feet tall with no barbs or barbed wire. Honestly, we had tons of time to make the escape, we were just high off adrenaline.

I climbed first and straddled the fence and offered a hand to Ana.

She gave me a snide look and said. "I know how to climb a fence."

I was dumbfounded. For almost a month I had only heard her talk once as a whisper, and now she was giving me a smart ass remark.

What she didn't know how to do, was swim. She had only been to pools and lakes a few times in her life. She was afraid of water, so preferred to read rather than frolic in the water with her imbecile foster families.

The woods got thicker and greener, one big salad. Ana had stopped to catch her breath. I tried getting her to run some more.

"What's the hurry? No one is coming after us at this point." She said.

"You're right." I said.

We walked hand in hand. We kept looking at each other, smiling.

"Why would you want to pretend to be mute?" I asked.

Ana always took her time when answering a question regardless of the weight behind it. This often reminded me of Dr. Pavlovich. A Psychologist's trick.

"The Jains believe that language is inherently violent, I believe that. It started as my own personal vow of silence. Then I realized that people don't like to be inconvenienced with mutes and deaf people. So they keep communication to a minimum. I didn't have to deal with people as much. Until you came along." She said. "And it gave me power over those orderlies that my voice never did. People in power do not like to be over-powered. Men hate when women do it. It's no different with those orderlies."

We heard the river and the highway in the distance and felt safe. I stopped her, hugged and kissed her. As safe as we were, we had to get to my brother, otherwise we would have made love right there in the woods.

We had to cross a river to get to the highway. I knew about the river and figured it couldn't be deep, for the most part it wasn't.

We were crossing slowly in waist high water, the current was strong and there were tons of big rocks to avoid. I held Ana's hand and she walked next to me. She stepped on a larger rock I had just avoided. She slipped and the current started to take her. I braced myself against a rock. She went underwater for a second. I pulled her up to me and carried her out of the water.

Chapter 16: The Conception of Ana

Ana was conceived in the most heartfelt and passionate way, in a calm before the storm as they say. Somewhere near the end of her embryonic stage, the shitstorm of human drama came through and ripped the love and serenity away.

Her mother was a beautiful woman named Jacquelyn Mary Murphy. She had learned the power of her beauty at a very young age.

Jacquelyn, never Jackie, and her friends would go downtown every weekend and sift through the classy discos for wealthy young men. Her friends were shortsighted and naive. They would often let any man take them to their hotel rooms. They would let these businessmen do whatever they wanted, all in hopes to land a successful husband. Mostly what they found were pompous rich kids, fresh out of pre-law school. Trust-fund babies equipped with the creepiest sexual fetishes.

Unfortunately, for these young women, they would submit themselves to all sorts of obscure sex acts only to be booted out at dawn, often finding out that these rich men were already married or engaged. 'Don't let the door hit your ass on the way out'. They would try this again and again with the same results.

These poor girls would end up miserable, until they found the revolving door of liquor and drugs and television.

Even Ana's mother was duped, and she was the smart one of the bunch.

Ana's mother knew that sex was never the way to make a man fall in love with her. Quite the opposite, she knew that holding out on the forbidden fruit makes the man all the hungrier. For several months, she had no success. She had a difficult time finding someone that she wanted. She watched her friends whore themselves out for a few martinis and a promise. The only difference was that real prostitutes didn't make believe they were princesses waiting for their charming princes. Fifty bucks and out the door you go. The oldest profession confused with the oldest non-profession, the wealthy housewife.

One day, Jacquelyn met a brilliant and powerful man, tall and handsome, her ideal. His name was William Phanes. She couldn't find a flaw with the guy. Little did she know. He was a trust fund baby, an heir to the ungodly fortune of the Phanes Porcelain Corporation.

More often than not, when you wash your hands, you'll see a little sun logo with a *phi* symbol inside stamped somewhere on the porcelain. The Phanes Porcelain Corp. dominated the porcelain industry, so much so that if you see any other logo, the Phanes Porcelain Corporation owns those companies.

William, this handsome trust fund monster, played the part of a pauper who worked hard at what he had earned so far. His career as a lawyer was excelling, and he had only been out of law school for a year. This wasn't because he was talented. It's about who you know, and what you have. Also, William was a good liar, with that skill you can go far in life, especially as a lawyer.

What really sold Ana's mother more than anything was how he had sexually held out on *her*. That had never happened. After a month of courting (this was mainly on the weekends, he lived out West). He told her he was saving himself for marriage. Jacquelyn was awed by this. How can a handsome and wealthy 27-year-old hold out that long? She should have trusted her gut, but she didn't. She loved him to death, or so she thought.

They went through the whole charade. It was so seamless and flawless that Jacquelyn only questioned the entire situation *because* it was perfect, too perfect. William proposed to her with the quintessential American engagement ring, the gold one with the ridiculously large diamond. He was on one knee, hand extended, eye contact. He was trained from birth to lie, he was rich. He was human.

The ring was worth a year's wages of any first-world factory worker. It was probably worth ten years wages of hundreds of people in the third-world from which that diamond came from. Many years later, Ana's father would be sent to prison for being part of a conflict-diamond trafficking ring with that same wedding ring used as a piece of evidence. He couldn't wait for his parents to die to inherit their fortune, they were far too healthy for their age. William wanted to make his own personal empire.

In prison he would have a chance to redeem himself as a loyal spouse. There, his spirit would be broken. It didn't take much, the prison he was sent to was more like a country club. But the confinement and public embarrassment led him to show his true colors. He would find out deep in his psyche that he truly wanted to be a woman.

Months after a wonderful wedding and honeymoon, Ana was conceived. Shortly thereafter, Jacquelyn got a phone call from William's mistress Lena, otherwise known as his high school sweetheart. Lena had hired a private detective to see why Will was being so weird and infrequent with his visits. She was finishing med school and planning to move back home so she and William could start their lives.

Jacquelyn was defensive and incredulous at first, but Lena got through to her. She filled her in on very important details such as flight itineraries and very particular sexual fetishes that gave it all away. William liked to wear women's underwear and get spanked.

This was all Jacquelyn needed to hear, and she didn't have much more to say to the woman who had been screwing her newly wedded husband.

She had absolutely no way of getting a hold of William until he called her, and when he did, the wrath of a woman slighted was unleashed. The first half of the conversation was frigid, Jacquelyn stewing. The second half was an indiscernible pulse of screams and profanity. Will sent her to her hometown the next day. Jacquelyn saw, not looked at, him once after that, to get the marriage annulled.

She didn't want money from him. What she wanted was for him not to be in their child's life. She didn't want his name on the birth certificate. He could live with that.

She wanted to erase the thought and memory of him. No pictures, no words. And she accomplished this. But as with all things traumatic that get suppressed, her fury would only grow. She became an ever-erupting volcano, her pain and anger bringing the carnage of lava and smoke. Ana became the little innocent town that gets buried and burned alive.

For nine long and torturous months, Jacquelyn lay in an emotional coma, a sleeping dragon. For nine long months, Ana would grow and grow, nourished by sorrow and resentment. She slept in a placental firebed, the byproduct of an immaculate deception. Her umbilical cord siphoned tears. Ana's spirit was born in her mother's womb, a cradle of devastation. She would be born into a world of hatred and deceit, not love and trust.

Ana was born as Jennifer Anne Murphy. She never used Jennifer passed the age of eight then she used Anne or Annie until age twelve. After that, she would always be known as Ana.

Ana the Anorexic.

It's a mother's instinct to comfort a baby's cry, and Jacquelyn lacked those instincts. She proved to be an awful mother. Everyone speculated she had postpartum depression, which was true. But it didn't matter much, no one could do anything about her. Her depression only worsened and changed forms, and Ana would become the victim of it.

The only kindness Ana would receive in her first year of life was from her grandmother, who died shortly after Ana's first birthday. Her grandmother, Ana would say, was probably the only reason she still had compassion. Jacquelyn started in on drugs and heavy drinking not a month after Ana was born. Lucky for Ana, the lack of her mom's motherly instinct had her on a formula diet. She was just lucky enough to be fed the concoction of simulated sugars and proteins made by the all powerful Nastomon, ruler of the sweetener industry. And luckier still that Ana's grandma was the primary caretaker, almost every night. Ana's drunk and high mom wouldn't have the chance to roll over on her while they co-slept. Lucky indeed.

Ana grew up around constant yelling and with herself crying and punished for being half of what her mother despised the most, her father.

She had no friends, rarely played outside. Imagine a girl at the age of five, institutionalized. She would find solace in school and books and writing. And she would find rebellion in her refusing to eat.

For the first time in her life, she had power over something. She had power over herself and her own well-being. This is when Ana made the decision to not eat meat. Denying food and in particular meat products would lead to beatings and imprisonment in her room, but her room was no longer a prison cell. It was her gateway into safer worlds, the worlds in books, and her escape from the reality she suffered from.

Every day, she would fill her backpack with books. Every day she would read and write, alone and sometimes starving. School teachers would often try to intervene on Ana's apparent negligent household but to no avail. This would always make her situation worse, but at least her mother never thought to take away her books or paper and pens. Ana remembered thinking during those times that if she were to suffer that punishment, she would find a way to die, by hunger if need be. This was a six year old thinking of suicide.

By the time she was eight, she was completely self-sufficient. And besides random, violent episodes with her drunken mother, things went smoothly. She had a few friends and got good grades, until she was awakened one night by one of Jacquelyn's many bar boyfriends.

She was frail and small but had the ferocity of a dragon. These dirty calloused fingers that were groping this precious and innocent eight-year-old girl, would be halted by tooth and nail and a fiery heart. Dragons beget dragons.

She bit his face and his neck until her teeth touched each time. Razor sharp dragon teeth. He was trying to escape, his blood everywhere. This monster of a man would soon look like a monster.

Monstrum in fronte, monstrum in animo.

Monster in face, monster in soul.

This would be the last time Ana tasted flesh of any kind. She had said that if she had to though, she would eat a human before any other animal. But to eat the world's worst creature was still sacrilege, she would rather die.

She had likened eating a human to eating a Chimera or a pig-vulture made to look like a hairless monkey or anything unholy and crazy.

The sexual assault quickly exposed the neglect that she was made to swallow at the hands of her mother. Social workers investigated every bit of Ana's life. They found everything, all the reports by teachers, all the drugs in the house, the filth that the house was covered in.

Only one room was clean in that house, Ana's room, which was covered in blood when they saw it.

The only thing that wasn't fully true was that Ana *was* fed, in a way. She was malnourished. This was due to her occasional refusal to eat anything at all, and her absolute refusal to eat meat. But to Ana, it was completely true, she went along with it. Her mother served meat more frequently once she knew Ana was against it. Ana felt justified in that.

Ana was justified.

The man who tried to molest her went to a jury trial to try and prove himself innocent. But Ana was there for it all, right up to his sentencing hearing. He got off lighter than he should have. Ana was disgusted, everyone was disgusted.

Ana was sent to stay with one of her aunts for a short time, and then another aunt and uncle, and finally another uncle. This would go on for three years. Her cousins would despise her and she them. She never had her own room and this would torment her. She would barely make a friend at school and she'd be uprooted again. She got accustomed to the solitude, the crying and the anger, and the numbness.

Each household turned out to be such a nightmare of conflict that the last possible relative wouldn't give it a try.

Almost every issue stemmed from Ana's eating (and non-eating) habits.

Ana's uncle was finally the one to spill his guts to the social worker about Ana's anorexia. Ana was sent to her first treatment center. She was the youngest one there, and she learned everything the older kids did.

Her life from then on would be a revolving door of foster homes and treatment centers. Most of the foster families were wealthy, and though patient, still sent her off for treatment. During that time, she became a ballerina and a pianist and a drug addict.

Once upon a time, Ana loved amphetamines.

Chapter 17: Broken Toilet

Everything changed with the liberation of Ana's voice, the tables were turned so to speak. I was used to having a dominant way of speaking to Ana when she was writing back.

Ana's voice was so beautiful and powerful that it made one forget how slender and fragile she was. This voice was the representation of her character, her ineffably strong and independent spirit. On the contrary, I perceived my own voice to be recessive. Unless I was angry, then I sounded like a lunatic which was nothing more than a grown child throwing a tantrum with words.

We walked hand-in-hand through the woods, parallel with the highway, until we reached Cy and his car. His car, or his true girlfriend as he'd sometimes call it, was a 1969 Mercury Cougar. We were in a sixties movie with greasers and preps and muscle cars and diners. He was leaning on his classic Cougar with his greaser hair, white T-shirt, and blue jeans.

My brother stood there with a smoking cigarette angled in his smirking grin. He welcomed us into his car.

The sun was dipping and making blue and red madness in the sky, the clouds like cream puffs. We approached Cy's house through the alleyway. This neighborhood tried desperately not to be a ghetto. It was called River Heights and earned its name because it happened to be on the side of the river that was some sixty feet higher than the other side. It was snug between the slums and the University, a perfect harbor for radicals of all types.

This neighborhood was bohemian and unique to the city, where many involved in counterculture took part in their rebellions of normal society. There were hippies and activists, punks and junkies, pretty much every sub-culture really, and the occasional violent revolutionary. They were all for the most part peaceful, and they couldn't shake the violent nature of the gangs. Most indigent were interwoven with them, but the gangs never stopped with the drugs and violence. Because the nature of love and equality, most people didn't complain of being robbed at gunpoint every couple months. These people believed in their community, and they led by example.

I knew this part of town well. A lot of my friends used to frequent the cafes and underage parties around here. The cops had too many problems with gang violence and armed robberies to worry about underage drinking and counterculture shenanigans. This was also Ana's third home, if treatment centers were her second.

Cy pulled into the space next to the garage.

Most of these houses were all the same. Steeple-pitched roofs on two-and-a-half-story duplexes. They looked like upside-down ships with no bow. The colors were what you'd find in the toilet, the shitty browns and the piss yellows and the puke greens. Half-ass fix-it jobs all over the place. Ragged enough to look squalid yet fixed enough to be habitable.

In the yard next to Cy's yard were countless cats. The neighborhood catlady, Judith, lived next door. Years ago, people would complain to the city about Judith's myriad cats, and the local pound would come capture what they could. But the neighborhood had the beginnings of a rat infestation and Judith's cats came to the rescue, eliminated the threat in short order. People were so worried about The Black Plague during that brief time that they never pestered poor old

Judy again. But her cats bred uncontrollably, and their main predator wasn't natural, it was the motorized vehicle. Their second predators were preternatural, the prepubescent boy with flammables.

Cy gave us the grand tour of the kitchenette, bathroom, dining room, front room, and his room. Most of his décor was vintage artifacts from the 50's and 60's, all that greaser rockabilly stuff. The spare room was what they used to call the maid's den which was nothing but half the attic with a partition and a door. But the one benefit was the sink and toilet annexed to the den. I was fine with the whole setup. Besides being a filthy mess, the toilet had a moldy curtain for privacy.

Ana didn't care.

"The toilet's broken, but we'll fix it this weekend. It needs a new float." Cy, much like my father, liked to include me to fix things. This meant that he would be fixing while I watched and handed him tools. "I was thinking of making a sand pit in the backyard for wrestling."

"Can we start tomorrow? I need to get back in shape." I asked.

"Couldn't you use that space for a garden or something a bit more peaceful? A pit full of sand is just going to be a litter box for all those cats I saw next door." Ana said.

"Jake's got his senior season coming up this winter. He has to keep up with his training if he wants to win." Cy said.

Ana put her head down. "Can I lie down somewhere?"

Although I could tell she was irritated with us, she was also very tired. Even with the added weight of the last few weeks she was still very skinny. And because of her body frame, she had the look of helplessness, though she was nothing of the sort.

She was clutching my arm in that precious form of affection a woman gives her man as a protector, but I knew that this was simple affection on her part. I didn't want her to let go but I insisted that she lie down and take a nap on the couch. She did so without another word.

"Let's start getting a place situated for you." Cy said, pulling out a couple of beers. He tossed one at me.

I caught the beer and thought of the calories then cracked it, nothing I couldn't get rid of later. "Are you sure it's okay that me and Ana stay?"

"I wouldn't say anything about rules but I know how it is being on your own before high school's finished." He took a huge swig. "I already made that mistake. My diploma is from prison." Another swig and he crushed the can and threw it in the sink.

My brother's rules were simple. Clean up your own shit, get a job and pay what you can, and most of all when school starts, I would have to go. He really didn't expect me to pay anything, so long as I helped him fix up the place. He just wanted me to hand him money to teach me some responsibility with finances. Our father taught us that money is a lie and nothing but a firestarter after Apocalypse, something not worth saving. Gold coins though, were worth their weight.

He had a spare bedroom which he'd been using as a storage room. We set about moving it all out to the garage as soon as we got there.

He was indifferent about Ana. He probably had the hunch that she wouldn't eat him out of house and home. But then again, he was indifferent about everything after he got out of prison. 'It is what it is', he'd always say. I would never see him get worried or anxious. 'What are they going to do? Send me back to prison? Be my guest, it's a prison out here.' This was one of Cy's mottos.

"Here's forty bucks. There isn't much food in here so feel free to order something. And don't be shy about it Jake. Let me know if you need money or anything. My house, your house." Cy said and sprinkled half his pack of cigarettes on the table.

He often said Spanish phrases into English. He taught himself Spanish in prison and literally translated Spanish idioms and sayings. One of his favorites was 'Go with God' for when saying 'goodbye' instead of *'Vio con Dios'*.

He told me where his home bar was, The Cornerstone, and that he'd be back at bar close. On his way out he said 'Go with God' and laughed. He was the epitome of atheism, but these types of things humored him. Half of his prison tattoos were religious, and he'd explained why, 'because what fun is life if you can't laugh about everything?' 'Far too serious', he'd also say, when someone didn't laugh at a very taboo religious joke.

***

Toilets are an ancient thing. Before human's thought to invent such a clever device to take away their urine and feces and vomit and menstrual waste, they had to disperse these wastes throughout the forest in holes, or in bowls which were dumped in the road.

Humans had long invented cheese and beer before they found a regular place to stow their shit. Toilets were invented around the time of the wheel, an invention of more importance for mankind at the time. What good is a chariot or a mill when your village is knee-deep in excrement that makes your people deathly ill?

In more modern times, late 16th century, a man by the name of Sir John Harington is credited with the modern flushable toilet. So much so, that Americans still call it 'The John'. Sir John called it Ajax and his fellow Brits would call it 'a jacks'.

Ajax was one of the heroes of the Trojan War who killed himself. Now Ajax is a cleaning product used on toilets and sinks. You will know that Ajax has been in to your house when it is the only pristine white house on a block of piss-stained ones. One man's legend is another man's cleaning product. At the FTC, Ajax would have been diagnosed with Severe Depression Disorder and prescribed Freshax.

My brother's attic room had a closet-sized bathroom with only room for a toilet. The toilet hadn't been flushed since he moved there and had a pale layer of hardened scum that held the vile stench of year-old bodily waste. I had to clean the thing before Cy would inspect what was wrong with it. Nobody has to be bulimic to toss cookies when cleaning such a vile mess.

After all my effort to clean the porcelain throne, my brother insisted on getting a new one. He had friends who could get him one for little or no money. Cleaning latrines lends itself to humility, like Gandhi, but cleaning a toilet that is being discarded anyway is just humiliating.

***

We walked, arms around each other, through the rows of homes. Here and there, people were arguing or praising in a drunken stupor, people were singing to themselves or with others, and people were watching and listening quietly at passers-by and the background din of human drama or comedy on the television.

We were both silent for awhile.

"Is it that strange to hear me talk?" Ana said.

"Yes, but in a good way. I like it, I like your voice. I don't know what to say right now."

"We have all the time in the world. Don't feel rushed." She looked up and squeezed me.

We headed to the main strip of the neighborhood, a bizarre mixture of liquor stores, cafes, re-sale boutiques, corner bars, and two fancy restaurants.

The restaurants were the wealthy people's window on diversity of the underbelly of American society. To them, it was like the average person's trip to the zoo to see the mysterious and interesting habits of foreign creatures. One of these restaurants was called the Epicurean, not at all philosophically related to its namesake, Epicurus, my employer for the summer.

"I used to live there." Ana said while pointing at a rotten paint-chipped house. So and so used to live there. 'I was at a basement show there.' 'Ex-boyfriend used to live there.' Ana knew the place well, and I wondered how many ex-boyfriends she had.

We stopped at a corner store, a liquor store that sold instant food and cigarettes.

We were both seventeen, Ana's birthday was in two months, but she had no problem buying cigarettes. In fact, she had been buying cigarettes from this store since she was thirteen. She knew the owner and all of his brothers and cousins. They were from Pakistan, and she spoke to them in Urdu.

She knew everyone, this guy and that guy, an occasional girl. This guy would give her a hug and that guy would smile and wink.

"Ex-boyfriends?" I asked. I was jealous, childish.

"A few." She clinched me. "You shouldn't worry, I have you. That's all I want."

If anything can be classified as wisdom, it's knowing and trusting when a girl tells you something sincere. The teenager (human) is unwise and full of doubt. I was the archetypal teenage boy.

As young lovers, we tend to foolishly trust people who are untrustworthy then in turn are incredulous to obvious signs of sincerity. I was gauging every guy that got a free grope on Ana. I wasn't physically threatened by any of them. I was intimidated by the unknown. In this case, it was a whole counterculture that I only knew of, from the outside. And this was Ana's home away from home away from home.

We got the cigs and I wanted food. When we were locked up in the FTC everything was served on a schedule and Ana was pretending to be a mute. So when it came to me ordering food, Ana started with a drop of the flood of her convictions.

It started with, "You don't need food, you have me." She was being playful. I wasn't very playful in response. I was terribly famished, the pangs only lasted for a small while. My love for her did override my desire to fill and spill a greasy pizza. This would go on for days, she would teach me the ways of the hunger artist, the starving spectacle of denying all that is wrong with the world. And to Ana, this was everything human.

On that hot damp night, she lit my cigarette, then hers. She took one drag and coughed and sprinkled the cherry on the ground. "I'm done. I've been done. I told myself after the last stint of freedom that smoking was frivolous and pointless, even if you're growing and smoking your own."

Ana was conscious of the cigarettes she bought, regardless if the tobacco was organic and the cigarettes were hand rolled by locals. This was the first and last thing I ever saw her buy. She only traded her work or bartered her own goods, for anything, which didn't amount to much.

She liked to call this rejection of buying any particular product, or anything for that matter, *deprogramming*. This was always in reference to how we are trained from birth to consume everything and unless we break that programming, the world will be exhausted.

I, on the contrary, hadn't understood how much I consumed. Ana was there to point it out to me, nearly every time. I loved smoking in the summer and chewing tobacco during the other seasons. I also loved to drink booze and beer, but with Ana around this would become a problem. She forgave all addictions (once upon a time, an amphetamine addict herself), but she was very open with criticizing peoples' vices. At first.

They told us at the FTC in Group that your main addiction will surpass all other addictions. For that first night and the few weeks to follow, Ana and I were addicted to each other and nothing else. I didn't care about food or cigarettes or beer. Ana was my divine drug, my sustenance and providence.

She told once that she could operate on pure spirit, and I didn't doubt her. For those first two weeks in her arms every night, I was free and existing purely on spirit, and my love for her. Passion has a stomach that can never be filled, so true lovers have this tendency of devouring each other.

But like most lovers, my euphoria only lasted a short while and my only reminder would be the bitterness of the memories of my lover lost. My human nature to destroy all that sustains me would reign. Just like almost every modern human on this planet.

My petty perceptions from my navel in the universe were too ignorant and pompous to see or listen to anything Ana had reached out with. I would become Orpheus. The human in me would ruin everything.

I understood later in life that we deal with our lover's hells as well as our own. When fiery love abounds, everything divine and demonic comes out. And I was young, but I take none of my rational or circumstance as an excuse. I would never release myself from the guilt, no matter the strength of my emotional fortress. Let me never forget! Let a vulture eat my alcohol-soaked liver for till the end of days!

***

The moon sliced white light through the dirty attic window. We made love several times in that moonlight on a squalid mattress and sheet. Our limbs like snakes writhing.

I was lying on my side running my fingers along Ana's face and body, absorbing everything. She had several tattoos, dark and sketchy like prison tattoos.

On Ana's back was an Egyptian scene with hieroglyphs underneath it. There was a scale weighing a human heart against the feather of truth with the Jackal-headed god Anubis standing in front of it. This was out of the Egyptian's Book of the Dead. She told me it symbolized the Conscience being weighed against Truth. The hieroglyphic prayer beneath it, Ana said, is one of the oldest in the world. "It's about people asking for forgiveness, though they've been destroying everything since they started. That's why I have the feather heavier than the heart. Truth weighs far more than our consciences. And we should all be devoured by The Eater of the Dead."

On her chest was a profile of St. Catherine of Sienna. Ana called her the Saint of Starvation. This was one of her role-models, and she made it very clear that she wasn't Christian because of it. She admired and felt akin to the story of St. Catherine. Catherine of Sienna had stood up to her father and men with starvation to be a conduit of God for the poor. Ana found strength in that Saint.

On her belly was a lotus and inside it was an inverted triangle with a snake coiled around a pill shape. She called it our 'root place', the source of our existence. I asked her why the egg was pill shaped.

"It's not an egg. It's a lingam stone, symbol of the phallus. The serpent is the female aspect in this symbol." She said.

I ran my fingers over her chest several times and her nipples. Her aureola were dark and bumpy. They were much different than the last time we made love at the FTC, and I was ignorant of what that meant.

"I'm pregnant." Ana said.

"How do you know that?" I said.

"You know. Can't you see the difference in my aureola?" She said.

"They seem different, but that doesn't mean much." I said.

"It means a lot. I know I'm pregnant. There's no doubt." She said. "We'll talk in the morning. Let's get some sleep."

Chapter 18: Eating for Three

I couldn't sleep and neither could Ana. We writhed like snakes, but without sex. I felt awkward and speechless and hungry. The thought of a baby in Ana's belly pleased me, but I was scared and confused. I avoided touching her belly, I didn't know what she thought. After I heard my brother leave for work, I got up and started getting dressed.

"I must have started ovulating when we first had sex." She said. She was putting her bra on, her breasts barely fit. "They were forcing me to eat more around that time. When you first saw me, they actually started breaking me down."

I told her I didn't understand and she went on to explain how anorexia and menstrual cycles don't mix. The body shuts that system down until it's nourished again.

"What do we do?" I said. This was a broken record in my head?

"We have to talk. And we have all day to do that."

"I have to get a job. I planned on it anyway, but now it's a little more urgent." I said. I felt cool on the outside, but I was overcome with anxiety. My mind was a blender full of scenarios. I wasn't done with school yet. I had to get a job and a place and a car. I was so far from all that. I had just gotten out of a glorified sanitarium.

"You need to know more about me first. I've learned so much about you during our time at FTC, but I didn't get to tell you very much about who I am, what I feel and think." She said.

I turned the light on in the bedroom. She moved to pull the shade up then turned the light back off. "You don't need the light on when there is perfectly natural and free light right there."

She looked so pretty in the dusty sunbeams, and her voice was sweet and strong.

"Let's go down to the river and talk." She said.

"I have to eat something first." I dug around the fridge, some eggs, milk and cheese and butter, some meat, a half-loaf of bread, and a bunch of condiments. "It looks like there is only bread for you in here. You want some toast. There's probably peanut butter and honey somewhere in the pantry."

She shook her head and watched me from a seat at the kitchen table. Her anger was barely contained. I was gathering utensils and ingredients.

"I think I'll wait in the bedroom until you're done with your chicken fetuses." She shut the door behind her.

I was cracking eggs in a bowl. "I'm sorry." I never thought of any of these things. I was completely detached from what anything really was. Eggs were food. Milk was drink. Meat was food. I was ignorant to every value that Ana held dear.

I whipped up a cheese omelet and slurped it up. I knocked on the door. "I'm done."

No answer.

"I'm really sorry. I never thought of it that way. I didn't know."

She opened the door and looked at me, her eyes crazed. "You're telling me that you didn't know how chickens are born?"

"Yes, I know that, but I never put it in perspective." I said.

"I forgive you, but you need to start thinking about these things. When you eat eggs, do you even know where they come from?" She said.

"Chickens."

"Don't get me started." Ana said.

***

You don't even want to get Ana started.

Don't get her started about poultry, about the beakless and clawless chickens pumped with steroids and virtually motionless until death, though the darkness of their world was death to begin with. Their tomb was their egg. And don't even mention snatching chickens' fetuses for your morning omelets.

You don't get her started about veal and the calves that are locked in little boxes for their short pitiful lives before being sent to the slaughter. You don't mention pate and the geese that are force fed with tubes. And don't bring up the bourgeoisie that eat these so called delicacies.

You don't want to mention silk and the worms that get boiled alive for their product and what Ana called 'Cyclical Holocaust'.

And don't mention the holocausts and genocides that happened or are happening worldwide. Don't mention what people can do to people. She wouldn't even get herself started about War and how it's the only thing that mankind does well, the ultimate display of its sickness

You might accidentally bring up farming and vegetarianism, but you don't want to get her started on that either. Corn and soy were ancient and precious things to Neolithic people that now have turned into Frankenstein versions of food that was intentionally used to produce poisons for you and your children, worldwide.

"People think they're Gods externalized, yet they know nothing of God and Gods internally." She would say if you mentioned religion. But you don't want to get her started on that, because then she'll be started on War.

And if you got her started about farming in general, she'd tell you that it has always been destructive to the planet, loss of animal's habitats and mass breeding of the biggest virus of all, humans. So you don't want to mention McMill's slashing and burning rainforest for your crappy fast food burger and all the cows that get decimated in the five industrial abattoirs, yes, five titanic slaughterhouses to feed the superfluous American *panphagic* tragedy. And you don't mention the Ozone or the poorly treated immigrants who get hired by faceless and soulless corporations who care nothing of a human or animal life, only money and power.

Don't start about sweatshops and migrant workers and child labor, and make no mention of pesticides and herbicides and the corporate destroyers like Santomon who make them. The same destroyer that sold you that ice cream for your kid and will sell your teenagers poisonous cigarettes, and incidentally the same corporation is owned in conglomeration with the pharmaceutical company that makes the pill that you're crazy teenager will have to take after being locked up in a treatment center, also owned by that same corporate destroyer.

Don't get her started about governments and newspapers and propaganda. Please don't.

You don't want to mention dairy farming and the perpetual cycle of yanking a cow's tits for a calf's life support while the calf eats the high fructose corn concoction totally severed from its mother just so you can have your milkshake, extra thick. Never mention animal testing or the chemical branch of Proxy and Keno. Don't bother.

If you mentioned hunting, she would ask you, 'how would you like it if someone came shooting at you every year when you wanted to go have sex?' You wouldn't like it. 'But humans do that to themselves anyway, and they call it *War*.'

And never ever get her started on Television. Ana would tell you that it is the epitome of the morally weak and corrupted human society, a syringe of stupidity and a friend to the apathetic friendless masses.

I had got Ana started more than once on more than one thing.

I honestly couldn't defend myself to her reasoning. She was right about many things, whether I believed them or not at the time.

***

"I have to make a stop before we go to the river." Ana said.

"Where at?" I said.

"I have to stop at a friend's house to pick up some make-up." She said.

"What for?" I said.

"I feel self-conscious without it. I'm fine when I'm in treatment, but when I'm not locked away, I need my mask to be social."

"But you're beautiful. You don't need that crap." I said.

"You're male, you don't understand about the pressures of society on women." She said.

"You lecture me about chickens and eggs, but you can't give up such a silly thing as make-up." I said.

"You don't know what I feel."

"I never said I did." I said.

We arrived at her friend Devi's house which was tucked in the ruins of abandoned factories along the river. Devi was an urban farmer. She had converted portions of these wastelands into viable farmland.

Ana left me by the gate of her house. Her irritation was simmering. She came back with a small satchel and some make-up around her eyes.

"You're beautiful." I said.

She shrugged.

We walked down to the river in silence. We followed a trail along the riverbank. Ana was picking up empty bottles and cans, candy wrappers and chip-bags.

“The world is sick Jacob. And it’s us humans that make it that way. We’re a virus.” She said picking up a glass bottle. She made a trash bag out of a large chip-bag that was fluttering on a branch in the wind.

I was contemplating helping her. She handed me the large chip-bag.

“I never wanted to bring a child into this.” She picked up a dirty syringe and tucked it into an empty bottle with a cap.

“So, you want to get rid of it?” I was flush.

“I never said that. I need to think about everything. I just want you to know that I never wanted children. It goes against everything I believe. There are too many of us as there is, it’s awful. Look at what we do.” She pointed at the pieces of trash hanging about everywhere.

I never really thought about abortion. In school, I always laughed at the people who took it seriously on either side. I never cared to be involved in such a sensitive issue.

“So, you want to get rid of it?” I said. I wanted to puke right there. I had held my omelet down in light of the pregnancy issue. I had already envisioned me dropping out of school and working full time. I thought about giving up bulimia and wrestling and my anger.

“I don’t know what I want.” She sat down on a rock and hugged her legs. I stood next to her and watched the debris float by. Aside from the trash, the river and trees were brilliant. It was getting hot and the dragonflies and butterflies were busy on the bank.

“You’re going to have to make up your mind soon.”

“You’re not going to tell me what to do.” She said.

“So I don’t have a say in this, do I?”

“No, you don’t.” She looked up at me. I wouldn’t look at her.

“I want you to understand how I feel, how bad this hurts me.”

I gave up talking. My anger was barely managed. I did not want to think about it any longer.

She had a lot of explaining to do. I was all ears.

Ana had been planning her personal revolution during this last stint in the FTC. She told me that the only kind of revolution left for us in modern America was a solitary revolution. This was due to the hyper-individualism that must be overcome to allow people to revolt as a community.

She hoped she could lead by example and influence others to do the same. She said that this kind of revolution was the only possible one for many of us, this generation of neighborly hatred. She despised violence and thought that most peaceful protests were useless. ‘We’re all hypocrites.’ She would often say.

“Everything is up for judgment. We are all guilty of something. We’ve caused this all. Men, women, and everyone in between. All of us, all this.” She pointed at the cars and roads, the buildings and houses, and the litter floating in the air. “And this is here, in America, this pretty paradise founded on death and exploitation. It’s nothing in comparison with the rest of the world. And we are all responsible.”

“To bring another child into this, I never wanted to do it. I’d be furthering this sickness of the planet, and the poor soul would have to go through the farce of this modern life. I’m confused. I don’t know what to do. If it were anyone else, there would be no question. I’ve already had an abortion when I was fifteen. It upset me at the time, but it made me truly realize that I didn't want to add to this mess. And to make another child suffer what I have suffered, that took away all my desire to breed."

"But I adore you Jacob, and my feelings for you make this all so confusing. If I wanted to carry a child to term, I would have to get over my anorexia. I'm so afraid that I can't do that."

Chapter 19: Revolution

"What is *your* revolution?" Ana said.

I was building a fire. We were on the riverside. Mosquitoes were grazing on Ana, she was gently swooshing them away. She wasn't Buddhist.

"Revolution for what?" I said.

"You need your own revolution Jacob." She was watching me. I could feel it. "Everyone needs a revolution. Gandhi had his revolution, he spun thread and picked up salt to show his people they could be self-sufficient and free of the British Empire. Che Guevara taught and healed, as violent as he was. Martin Luther King Jr. peacefully fought racism and to end segregation, the rotten core of our history," she said. "Jesus wanted all people to love and forgive each other. Though most of his followers continue to support wars and violence in his name, Jesus meant well with his revolution. He inspired so many other non-violent revolutionaries."

I was making a little nest of birch bark and tiny twigs. I lit a match.

"What would you like every human to do?" She said.

A flame burst from the nest with puffs of breath. As a kid, I was made to start fires in the most primitive ways. My dad felt that this one knowledge was the key to surviving the Apocalypse along with several others such as flintknapping and hunting and fishing.

"Everyone should know how to take care of themselves in a survival situation." I said. My father's son, the End Time Survialist.

I set the flaming bundle down.

"You should teach people how to build fire, to survive, to be self-reliant."

"Anyone can start a fire."

"Anyone can own a lighter." She said.

I built the fire up, twig after twig. I was always backtracking when talking to Ana. I knew what she was telling me, but it often took me awhile to make sense of it.

"I don't know how to start a fire with a lighter or a match." She knelt by me.

"It's easy really, if you use a lighter. Start small and dry then work your way up gradually. It's mainly about patience."

Actually, it wasn't easy for me when I was seven years old.

'When you start losing your teeth, you're old enough to start a fire and have a knife,' my dad told me.

Meanwhile, I got a glimpse of what I would go through by watching my brother try for hours to spin a stick between his hands. It took me years to learn the bow-drill method let alone the hand-drill method, and to think I had it easier than my brother. Cy gave me all the tips and tricks my dad wouldn't tell us. My dad was fond of not explaining much of what he was teaching, he believed in the way that some people learn Tai Chi or Qi Gong in China, where a student observes the master and learns to teach himself without explanation. 'The hard way is the best way', was my dad's motto for life.

"Easy for you. I want you to teach me, but I don't really want to start a fire." Ana said.

"How do you expect to learn if you don't actually try it?" I said.

"I just want the knowledge. I have no use for a fire personally. It's a destructive thing for man to possess. I understand the ease it brings to humans, but the violence of harnessing fire is rooted in mankind's prehistory and history, and that has led us to where we are now, nuclear bombs and televisions. My conscience won't allow me to go with it. I can't let myself smoke cigarettes anymore."

We sat next to the fire. I didn't want to talk. I just wanted to be next to her, but she had my mind churning.

"I think everyone should know how to make a fire and a tool from stone and wood," I said. "Making a tool isn't hard. It's in our instincts. Anyone could make a crude axe out a broken rock if they put their mind to it. So if anything, I would like people to think about all the things that they take for granted, like air and water for example. It won't always be so easy," I said.

"You need to teach people then. What use is knowledge, if we don't share it? I think that would be an excellent start to your revolution." She said. "You can start by teaching me."

I set some dead branches on the fire tepee.

"It's only natural that your revolution will be violent Jacob. But as long as you control your fire, I forgive you for that. You're a man, it's in your nature to destroy things. But I can only be tolerant of it if you can harness it."

***

I kept my thoughts and feelings about abortion and Ana's pregnancy deep inside my head. If there was something I was ever good at, it was burying emotions. At least for awhile that is, until everything explodes and spews forth.

For a week, we were perfect, holding on to the bliss. Ana adored me more than anyone before and after, for seven days. And I worshiped her. I listened to everything she said with stares from a sacred place. I felt like Odysseus when he was on the beach with Calypso. I was in a Time-less and Space-less existence, where a woman can envelope a man with the beauty of her spirit, and when nothing else exists.

But we were human beings, not gods or legends. We were stowed away in the Land of the *Lotophagi*, the lotus-eaters, stuck in a whirl of ecstasy, ourselves the dreamy lotus food. But here on Earth, reality always comes back somehow or someway, even if it means death.

During that flawless week, everything was simple. We spent much of our time down at the river, walking and talking. I resisted the urge to call my friend David up. I had successfully avoided the calls from my mother. My father only called Cy's house on Sundays when he came into town to trade his handmade goods for a week's supply of whiskey, so it wasn't very hard to avoid that call.

I only hung out with Cy once during that week, and that was to help him remove sod and lay sand.

Other than that, it was Ana's and my time, and I'll never forget it. For the rest of my life, when times are bad and lonely, I will shut my eyes and visit with my Ana at the river.

I didn't eat very much and didn't puke once. Sometimes I question myself if I made it all up, but then I come to my senses and know that it was real. I believe what Ana had said. 'The hunger goes away, and your spirit takes over. And you'll be able to talk to the God inside you.'

After that week, that dreamy state of lovers had to clarify. The lotus of ourselves of which we had been eating, softened its hazy effect.

We snapped out of it and bore all.

***

Ana forbade me to eat what she called "garbage". This was everything besides organically and locally grown fruits and seeds. She knew it was a huge leap for me, so she was tolerant. But I had to truly know where all of this stuff comes from. "Just know it. But not for pretend, like it's a slogan." She had said. She wanted us to plant a garden, if Cy let us.

It was a bright, hot day, and the city smells lingered. The summer sounds of cicadas buzzing and kid's playing in the hydrant spray, nobody drunk and fighting.

Ana took me to the local farmer's market in River Heights to meet her Indian friend Devi. As long as one could find Devi at the market place, one could tremendously reduce their guilt of destroying the planet and those around them.

Devi had the biggest stand at the market. She was always weaving on her huge loom. Every weekend she woke up at dawn and after yoga spent two hours assembling this giant wooden frame of the loom. Just to show people that they can do everything for themselves.

Devi always looked you in the eyes. If she was weaving, she would stop and address you fully.

She stopped weaving when we approached and offered her hand after Ana introduced us.

“Pick out some food Jacob. Whatever you want.” Devi told me.

“I don’t have any money.” I said.

“We don’t use money here, unless there is no other way. Just make me something for trade or come help me at my place sometime.” She said.

I was scanning the tables, overwhelmed. Besides the cornucopia of fruits and vegetables and spices, she had several different raw goods I was familiar with because of my father’s end of the world obsession. She had raw goods and finished products, papyrus and paper, oak galls and ink, flax and cotton and cloth, and ground indigo and henna for dying.

I walked around the farmer’s market while Devi and Ana talked about Jainism and the problems of the caste system in Hinduism.

Devi was raised Hindu but subtly converted to Omnism, she believed in Everything. She had issues with her native religion Hinduism, not the spirituality or wisdom, but the contradictions some of the tenets that were exercised by some sects and clergy. She believed in unity of all people.

I grew up going to farmer’s markets but not like the one in River Heights. My dad would have loved it. His do-it-yourself attitude (because apocalypse is nigh) was a perfect fit with the spirit of self-reliance in that neighborhood.

“Can I have some of these?” I asked Devi. She handed me a small burlap sack.

I grabbed a handful of cashews, some figs, and a pomegranate. I was intentionally eating slow, we were in public, and Ana was watching me as she kept her conversation with Devi.

On our way back home Ana and I were holding hands. I was carrying my burlap sack, and she was carrying a bundle of flax. We passed a couple walking with their children.

The mother was pushing a toddler in a stroller. The father had an infant strapped to his chest. The baby was sleeping, listening to his father's heartbeat.

I almost welled up with tears. That never happens. I choked on a swallow. We were both silent, instantly. Ana didn't look at the family. She stared ahead.

I pulled my hand away, she didn't resist.

I wrestled with myself about bring up the pregnancy. I decided to leave it alone and try not to think about it. Let Ana work it out for herself.

***

"How would you like to die?" Ana asked me. She was weaving a small basket out of river grass. I was digging a hole, scooping out the red river clay into bucket.

"I always wanted to die in a battle. Not with guns and missiles, but with spears and swords, like a Spartan or a Viking." I said.

"You men are silly. I'll never understand this obsession with fighting."

“What else is there for us to do? We fight and we make things and talk about making things. And we make things to fight or kill. Other than that we make babies, or pretend to make babies.”

I stopped to look at her. I was looking at her breasts and belly. Her face was focused on weaving, it had changed. I hadn’t realized the meaning behind what I said, until it was already in the air. Our voices went silent. The river talked, and I was mixing clay with water, the slopping sounded like wet sex.

“When I was younger, I wanted to jump into an Orca pool, and let it toss me around like they do with seals. But now, I think dying from starvation is the only way to go. I think my revolution would be discredited if I didn’t.”

“When you do that, please do it after I’m dead. I’d be a disaster now, so imagine in twenty years.”

“You’d be fine. People suffer far worse tragedies in life, and go on living wholesome lives.”

“ I don’t want to think about it.” I said. I was mixing the clay with water.

“You should think about it. It’s healthy. A great samurai once said that thinking about death all of the time can help you appreciate life. I think he was right.” She said. She finished her basket and started picking more reeds. “That looks like mudcake batter. Have you ever heard of a Haitian mudcake?”

“No I haven’t. What is it?”

“In Haiti, some people are so poor and starving that someone invented a recipe to make more cakes from half the amount of flour. They add mud to dough to make more cakes. They trick their bellies into thinking that they’re full. People actually sell these mudcakes. But they pay the price in the end. Mud can do horrible things to the intestines and that's not including the parasites. Some people die, just to feel like they are full."

"That can't taste good. Do they salt them?" I said.

She scrunched her eyes at me. "Have *you* felt real hunger?"

"I fasted for almost two days for wrestling, and every time my dad took me and my brother on vacation, we were starving by the end. Survival expeditions were my dad's version of a family vacation. And I went a day and a half without food just hanging out with you without even realizing it. Most times I don't care for it though."

"Fasting isn't hunger because you do it on purpose. There's a big difference. You've never been seriously hungry, deathly hungry. Maybe, you should think twice about bulimia." She said.

I was pushing the muddy clay through the screen with my fingers. Our surroundings filled the void of our dialogue.

"Not only do men kill each other, they sell each other too. You know all about slaves. We live in the land of slaves." She said. She was making a grass bracelet for me. "Haiti had one of the first modern revolutions. Now look at them. The people suffer the same but by the hands a different master. Now their masters look like them. And nobody cares." She walked over to me to watch. I was mashing clay through a screen into another bucket and picking out the pebbles.

"Nobody cares about anything except themselves. Maybe it's a male thing." I said.

"Everyone's guilty of this. You and I alike. But most of these people are disgusting."

"Am I disgusting?"

***

“We have to talk.” Ana said.

I was carrying the buckets full of wet clay. She had baskets in her hands. We were walking up the hill.

“We have been talking.”

“You know what I mean. We need to talk about our situation. I know it’s bothering you.” She said.

“I don’t want to talk. I really don’t care. That situation is your problem.”

“You do care. I know you do. But don’t you want to know what I think?” She said.

“Think whatever you want. It’s not my problem.” I wanted to take a break from carrying the buckets, but the pain was distracting my thoughts. I continued.

We went silent, all the way back to Cy’s house.

Some time passed before we spoke again. I just wanted to kiss her and hold her. That night we writhed like snakes sex-wise.

***

I woke from a dream that night and stumbled down to the kitchen.

I had dreamt of wrestling my father on top of a mountain in a lightning storm. He was drunk and easily maneuvered, and yet he was too strong for me to throw him down the mountain. Finally, he slipped and my mind changed to help him. He slipped from my hand and plummeted down the mountainside into a black abyss.

I woke up sweating and thirsty. I was chugging down water out of a gallon from the fridge when Cy walked in. I could tell he was hammered, but he could always keep his composure. He had the fortitude of an ox.

"The sandpit is finished. We have to start training you." Cy said.

"Can we make a garden on the other side?" I asked.

"Why not?"

Chapter 20: Starving Kids

When you're a kid and your mom tells you to finish your meal, because there are starving kids in Africa who would love to have the scraps off your plate, you feel bad at first. But deep down, like most children who haven't much of a conscience for people they've never met, you really don't give a shit. You just eat your meal to spare a kick in the ass from your father.

There are kids in Africa and India and so many other places in the world that are starving, and as a kid you'd probably fork over any uneaten or undesirable food to any frail kid with a paw out. You might wish that there were people that would clear your plate of any unwanted food like your groveling family dog. The starving kids would get a little bit of food, and you would be saved from getting your ass kicked. Win-win.

You can imagine a non-profit organization that specialized in such things as uneaten scraps of food from the affluent to the needy with clever names like LFFE (they would say it like 'life') Leftover Food For Ethiopians. But when you're a kid you don't know much about germs and decay, food preservation and distribution. In due time, somebody would finally rescue food and deliver it to the poor before it goes bad and into a landfill. As a kid staring at the unsavory remnants forcing yourself to swallow the cold Brussels sprouts and fat-chunks of a slice of ham is difficult, and then you remind yourself of your father's boot.

I found a job as a dishwasher at the Epicurean, a high class restaurant seated on the main street of River Heights. There's probably an 'Epicurean' in every artsy-fartsy neighborhood in every city in

America. You can wander through any one of these hodge-podge revolutionary neighborhoods and find this polished little gem of American greed and excess. A diamond in the rough. Imagine a Nazi five-star restaurant in the middle of a Jewish ghetto right before World War II, yet a bit subtler. It always reminded me of the zoo where spectators got to watch a day-in-the-life of such-and-such animal.

I learned a lot from these epicures that wined and dined there. Most of all was that their mothers hadn't reminded them of starving African children, and if those mothers did remind them, they didn't have fathers that would use a leather belt as a punishment.

I pulled in plates with barely two bites taken out of the entree or most of a bowl of chicken consomme. The portions were so small. I couldn't help but wonder how many of these rich people had eating disorders. There were cleaned plates on rare occasions. I could only assume that someone saved their change to afford a fancy night out with their date.

The Epicurean is named after a philosophy, which is named after the philosopher, Epicurus. When I told Ana that I had gotten a job there, she laughed and told me the story of Epicurus.

'I had to look it up after you told me you applied there. The meaning of Epicureanism as we know it in English is distorted and disturbing if we look to the source.' Ana had said.

Epicurus believed that one can attain *ataraxia*, which is a state of being absent from pain and suffering, by pursuing things that are good and do not cause pain. Nowadays people use Epicureanism as a term for eating and preparing gourmet food.

He also thought that there was no afterlife, and of this, Ana was very fond. She said to me, "People put too much weight on dying. Most people revolve their entire life around what their life will be when they're dead and not when they're actually living. They're programmed to think that nothing is cyclical, which is silly."

I always hated dealing with scraping plates at home when it was my turn to do dishes, but after being a dishwasher at a restaurant, I got over it. I made a meditation, a rumination of the knowledge being thrown at me from Ana and others. And I had been accustomed to dealing with the nasty half-digested food that left my mouth daily, this made dealing with leftover food easy as pie. What disgusted me most was that there were hardly any plates without a decent amount of food left on them.

The empty plates would remind me, of me. They were probably at the toilet, silently puking. It takes a lot to silence a good vomit. There were consistently dishes with barely a bite taken from them, they were like Ana but without a cause outside of themselves. It was like going to church without the notion of redemption, pointless.

I often wondered when and where you draw the line with a disorder. The obsession I had with getting rid of what I just ate was just as bad as counting every little calorie that was ingested. Everybody is guilty, plate after plate, partially eaten entrée after picked-at dessert, marathon-runner lawyer after waif model, bulimic wrestler after anorexic revolutionary.

And we were told about kids starving in third-world countries, and now some of us finish everything, eat anything, now we are that fat belly of American society. The working class. And fat is a bad word. To twist the knife in the fat gut, most of the food is beautified garbage, genetically modified and coated with poison and grown from oiled soil on the burnt remnants of a sacred rainforest.

I had my own ethical challenge working in the Epicurean. Since living with Ana, she had been teaching me more and more of the ailments of the world. It was like mom telling me about the starving Africans times a hundred. She knew it all. Every little tidbit about all the crimes of our obese American society. So, with her in my ear to create a conscience, like my mom making me finish my food, I had to reflect on what I was doing.

When the dishes came in at a slow rate, too slow to fill the Auto-washer 300, I went to watch the chefs or chat with the sous-chefs or line cooks or prep cooks. I already knew a bit of culinary arts but this was a divine opportunity.

As a co-worker of the Epicurean I was allotted a free meal per shift. I started off by just placing an order with Jacques or Chef Jeff and have them show me how to cook what I was going to eat.

Jacques was from France and moved to America at an early age. Most of his use of French consisted of swearing. He would call me *chef de plunge.* Besides French cuisine, he hated French culture. He hated culture in general. He would often say 'Culture is a group of people worshiping themselves. I forget who said that, but it is very true.' He was also an avid anarchist. About governments and religions, he would call them *merdé* or 'shit' in French.

Jacques was the only one who was allowed to do the puff pastry dough. His dad was a pastry chef, or *pâtissier* he would call it. He learned how to make this dough and many other things at an early age. He had never attended culinary school and had no desire to.

There were many other dishes and components that he had to make because he was French. He would say, '*C'est des conneries! (*'this is bullshit'), just because I'm from France, I have to do all the French things.' He'd also say to me when I would watch him rolling out puff pastry on a slab of marble. 'Nothing is hard, if you know what you're doing.' When someone complained about him, he'd say to everyone including the actual chef, John. 'Go ahead, fire me. How would you make Beef Wellington then, eh?'

Puff pastry in America comes in tubes or sheets at the grocery store. These forms are what the working class buy to make crescent rolls. Jacques had a theory that many of the customers of the Epicurean wouldn't know the difference between his puff pastry and the rolls on the shelves. He said only the filthy rich people and the chefs that make puff pastry can tell the difference.

Chef Jeff wasn't an actual chef. They called him that because his name rhymed with the title and because Jacques said that in French we are all *chefs,* even me. I took Chef Jeff's position and he moved up to a prep cook position. He would refer to me as 'Dish Pig', the same name he was called as a dishwasher, just like the person before him and on and on.

The real chef, John, who made the menu and occasionally checked to make sure everything was correct, spent most of his time sleeping in his office. He was always hungover. Regardless of his potbelly, he had a solid stature. He could have been a wrestler in high school or college, he had that *walk* of a person very able to defend themselves.

Chef Jeff called himself a *freegan*, or a person that will only eat animal products if it's free and going to waste. He had tattoos of dots and lines on his face. Also, he always had to wear a hairnet to cover his dreadlocks. The State's Health Department demanded this of him, and he would bitch about it constantly. More than once he'd ask everyone 'Isn't bureaucracy stupid, it was probably invented to give idiot cronies a job?' He personally knew Ana from over the years. He made it a point to tell me that he had never dated her, but he said I was a lucky man. I had often thought to ask Ana if she screwed him, but I was better off not knowing.

Chef Jeff talked only about food and socialism (and bureaucracy). He frequently told me a story he wrote called *The Farmer and the Doctor*. He wanted to write a children's book with that title. 'The Doctor only knows what he knows because the Farmer feeds him. The Doctor knows what he knows so he can heal the Farmer. It's as simple as that.' He had crude sketches and outlines of how to show kids about sharing and caring and equality without the bastardized usage of the term Socialism in America.

After some time I was allowed to cook my own meals. This turned out to be a culinary school in itself, and with the prep-cooks I learned just as much. I could have or make anything, a truffle roulade topped with crème fraiche or filet mignon in a buere blanc sauce, any meal I wanted.

I ate and drank like a king and puked like a plague-laden pauper, or did both like a Roman aristocrat. I got myself a feather for my emetic at work. I had no desire to get myself a spongia. Besides being good at torturing and conquering, the Romans knew how to make oneself vomit.

But then my conscience arrived with the knowledge fed to me by Ana.

***

All the time I spent with Ana, I felt famished. She encouraged me to eat all the fresh things from the market. I picked wild garlic and thimbleberries and dandelion greens to make salads. She never ate with me. "You already saw me eat enough times, it's embarrassing to me." She had told me.

I did some the stuff my dad taught me for surviving the Apocalypse like picking mushrooms and edible greens and nuts. I stripped the inner bark of maple trees to make noodles, but this didn't go over well with Ana. 'How would you like it if I removed some of your skin for a snack. Don't get me started.' That was her response to me doing that.

Eating like that, your stomach's a black hole when you're a spoiled brat. Although I was somewhat nourished with fruits and nuts, I was always hungry until I got to work. My days off were the longest and worst.

***

I always brought my toothbrush to work even after I found a decent feather to stick down my throat. I had to rid myself of the smell of cooked flesh. I was constantly paranoid about disturbing Ana in any way. Regardless of what I did, she was repulsed by me when I got home from work. I would get defensive and tell her that my job was to deal with food for eight hours.

I came home from work the one night, Ana was reading under a lamp, as usual. She burned through a book a day at least, and that was on top of all of her crafts.

She was reading *The Jungle* by Upton Sinclair. It's a book about the actual American Dream at the turn of the 20th century which consisted of all the awful things that are done to people when rich people don't have rules to follow. I hadn't heard of it at that time. And it was no wonder Ana was so irritable.

“What is that smell?” She said, “I’m sorry, but it makes me nauseous.”

“I didn’t eat any meat.” I said.

“It doesn’t matter. You smell like an abattoir. It fucking stinks.” She said. She rarely swore. *Verbal weapons* was her term for it.

“I’m sorry, it’s my job.” I was trying to decipher what ‘abattoir’ meant, had no clue. I thought it might be related to the Minotaur. I was too proud and angry to ask. I looked it up later and found out that it was a French word for slaughterhouse.

To avoid another scuffle, I went straight to the shower.

After I got out, she wasn’t reading *The Jungle* anymore. We were both calmed down.

“I’m sorry.” She came to me and hugged and kissed me. “I shouldn’t read that book if you’re going to be around. Or anyone for that matter. It’s that bad. People are that bad.”

“What’s it about?” I said.

“It’s a story about how bad people can treat other people and animals. You’ll just have to read it. I’d probably break down just telling you about it.”

“That bad?”

“Yes, that bad. It’s a window onto how horrible our species is. I picked it up for inspiration.” She said.

I didn’t read *The Jungle* until years later. I was shocked to find out how many people couldn’t finish it, and how many people didn’t want to describe it. People don’t like to know some of the bad things people do to each other. Some people said ‘That book is fucked up.’ This was no insult to Mr. Sinclair’s writing, he was just writing a fictional account of the realities of the immigrant worker before labor laws and unions, and that was what was 'fucked up'. What humans can do to other humans, let alone everything else.

"Where did you get it?" I asked.

"At Demos Book Co-op. I've worked there on and off for the past five years. I figured I should be working when you are, and honestly, that's the only job I think I can tolerate." She said.

"I've heard of it. Do they pay well?"

"It's voluntary until someone steps down from one of the few paid positions, but it doesn't matter." She said.

"I should be making enough to pay my brother rent. I think we'll be alright."

"We will be. And we don't need money, really. I can bring home books whenever I please so long as I bring them back." She said.

"Good. Because I feel like an idiot around you sometimes. I've never heard of some of these books you've read or the things you talk about. I just learned what socialism actually is. And to think I actually spent most of my life being told I was smart?" I said.

"Don't worry. Most Americans don't know what socialism is, they don't want anyone to know. They want everyone to be stingy little brats like the movie stars they are so in love with. And you know a lot more than you think, you just don't have fancy terms that scholars have for things."

***

Cy and I finished the sandpit. Judy's army of cats had already managed to start using it as a litterbox, although we covered it with a blue tarp to prevent that very thing. The tarp had piles of yellow puke-encrusted hairballs. I couldn't imagine what her house looked like.

I raked all the catshit that I could but still ended up with one in my face when by brother tossed me on my back and I rolled onto my stomach. There it was two inches from my face, a cat log.

The first few throws were vicious. The first stage of my training, my brother showing off.

If I had gained fifty pounds of muscle, Cy could out wrestle me any day of the week, except Sunday of course. Cy didn't believe in the Sabbath or keeping it holy, but he did believe he had the right to be lazy with the rest of God's flock on God's rest day. These kinds of things were how Cy dealt with the ghost of his Catholic faith. When starting a fire he would say. 'See, I can do things that God can do.' He was always fighting with my mom.

We started off wrestling full power, sweating instantly in the summer heat. This only lasted a few times of Cy pinning me. We then started my real training.

Cy went through move after move with me. He showed me all the mistakes I was making with my body throws. We sparred some more after that, but even with Cy at half strength and me struggling to grab his Goliath-like limbs, the spectacle looked like a cat playing with a mouse.

"Don't use all your strength at once. Stay loose, explode when the time is right. You should start running. You're getting out of shape already." Cy said.

I was.

***

When I started washing dishes, I shoved the leftover chunks of food down the Sinkerator, an enormous portal of food disposal. By the time I got fired much of it went down my gullet. The leftovers I would pick and choose to eat were far more than enough to break my 1600 calorie quota, and that's not to mention my free meal.

I wondered how different was it that I would lick my plate clean and send it off only a little more chewed. Yes, it all goes to the same place, just like us. No matter if it comes out of your ass or your mouth or never leaves your plate. But we are human and all of our ethics are derived by what we feel is comfortable with what our conscience has developed. As for mine in those times, I figured I had licked the plate clean and my mom would be proud. As for Ana, now that's a different story.

Ana disliked the concept of bulimia, the word itself, its origin. *Bulimia* was derived from the Greek word for the hunger of an ox. She thought it was the vainest and most wasteful eating disorder of them all, even worse than hyperphagia. She urged me to stop, if I cared about anything.

I resisted a little bit. She put me in my place and called me a panphagic or eater-of-all.

Omnivores are usually ignorant to vegetarianism or veganism, but self-proclaimed carnivores are more than ignorant, they somehow feel that vegetarianism is wrong and that everyone should eat meat and only meat all of the time. Most vegetarians will, at one time or another, have a pompous meat-eating asshole question the whole idea of vegetarianism. They'll ask 'Why?' and continue with false 'facts' and bullshit statistics to say that people are suppose to eat meat.

A sensitive and novice vegetarian will take this kind of thing too personally, get worked up, and lash out without a real defense. But a seasoned vegetarian can tear down an ignorant meat-eater. Same way a well-read atheist can tear down an ignorantly faithful born-again Christian, the way my half-Jewish friend David would.

The first time I saw Ana tear someone down, it was me. I had dared to question the things I did not know about, and this was to justify why I continued to eat meat.

"What are you going to do when the world ends, and you have to survive? Nuts and berries aren't going to cut it." I said.

"Don't get me started. Nuts and berries are plenty enough for me. But if all I had access to was meat, I would rather die. Then you have permission to go ahead and eat me. I'd make a good appetizer. My scrawny flesh might tide you and your murderous friends over until you can slaughter the next innocent animal."

"You would wither away and die on just the nuts and berries. You wouldn't be of much help to the tribe if you're frail and weak."

"What tribe? I don't need a tribe. A strong tribe gets too big and needs to settle and start farming to support more and more people, and after more and more people, the tribe across the canyon attacks you because they have the same problem as you do. All of a sudden, you have a city with nowhere to put you excrement and it spills throughout the streets. I don't want that. I am a tribe, and I don't need to destroy a planet just because I can. I can do everything I want up here." She pointed to her temple.

Anytime I got Ana started, I shut up and she didn't stop. She had deep-rooted convictions and I had to respect that. I, on the other hand, didn't have convictions.

***

I horrified her one day by bringing home a *filet mignon* and a winebox with two bottles of *pinot noir*. Again, I wasn't thinking.

After I got off work, I went and picked Ana up from the Demos Books Co-op to walk her home. The gunshots like an offbeat snare through a summer night were a constant reminder of how I didn't want her walking alone.

She didn't want to walk home either, she had friends both raped and robbed walking right on the fringe of the neighborhood. She could have walked home with one of her co-workers, but I didn't trust any of the male ones. I was a jealous boy, and they were idolizing vermin. And it gave me time to read some and spy on those vermin while I waited for her to get done with whatever.

She had settled in to read before bed. I pulled the meat from my survival sack, one of the bottles of *pinot noir* out of the winebox, a baggy of black peppercorns, some carrots and fingerling potatoes. I pounded the peppercorns on a cutting board with the side of my fist and rolled the steak in it. I fired up a sauce pan with a little oil and started searing the steak. My nose was smiling.

"What are you doing?" She said. She was enraged, I had never seen her face so distorted with anger.

"Uh." I had a fork in the meat, ready to flip.

"I thought I made myself clear the other day when you were frying chicken fetuses."

"I'm sorry, I just wanted to practice cooking. I didn't pay for it." I said.

"Doesn't matter. It's supply and demand. You're only adding to the demand, regardless of how you obtained it." She said.

I flipped the steak. She couldn't stay in the room. I could hear her in the other room softly screaming and babbling to herself. She sounded like a banshee under a blanket, she sounded crazy. I wasn't going to stop. The damage was done, or at least that's how I thought of it. So I continued to cook my *filet mignon* with red wine reduction. I had blanched the veggies for her with a sprinkle of salt and pepper.

Not only did I eat really fast, I had started eating very large bites with little chewing involved. Ana had made comments about bulimia and several of its fallacies. Though I refused to believe them without proof, I had developed my own theory of how I could reduce my caloric intake by having larger barely chewed bites in my stomach. So by the time I would puke, I wouldn't have digested as much as if I chewed them thoroughly.

I got the idea from a science experiment I had in middle school. We all had to put a chunk of steak in a jar of hydrochloric acid and document the results of a two week period. Judging by my experiment then, I definitely wasn't absorbing the amount of calories that Ana said I was.

When I was done, I went upstairs to our room. The lights were off, Ana was under the covers crying. I could hear the little sobs.

"I cooked you some vegetables."

"Fuck you." She went back to crying. The few times she swore, always at me.

Not only did I not cry for years as a teenager, I was also insensitive to it. I was my eschatologist father ignoring my crying Catholic mother.

"I'll put it in the fridge then." I said.

I was at the toilet, digesting the situation.

Throwing up large wads of meat is very difficult. It's like reverse choking, like the Heimlich maneuver. Sometimes it's too rough, you have to swallow it and try it again. This can become very disturbing which helps with getting it out. This kind of violent force that can be involved with vomiting can hurt other parts of the body. You can pop blood vessels in the eyes and face, pull or tear muscles in the chest and abdomen, mildly dislocate your jaw. Some snakes naturally dislocate their own jaw to swallow prey, and some also vomit on you when you pick them up.

There is a type of bulimia that involves regurgitation then swallowing or chewing again. It's like indigestion only worse. This can last several times for some people according to some eating disorder journal I read at Demos. It's called Rumination Syndrome. For some, their mouth becomes an additional stomach. Cows have four, humans typically have one. The light cases of this syndrome have harsh and chronic indigestion, but there are those that repeatedly puke and chew, puke and re-chew. Never met one of those types.

I sat at the kitchen table and drank the bottle of wine. Since leaving FTC, I hadn't thought about drinking much, Ana was my life. Even after having a few beers here and there with my brother, I hadn't felt the urge to get drunk. My euphoria with Ana was fading some, enough for me to start brooding about things I had been suppressing. I was drunk on Ana for those weeks and starting to get a hangover.

Dr. Mantha's Compedium of Myth Legend was open to the table of contents, I was drinking out of the bottle, browsing and looking at the loud clock intermittently, tick. I had a sharp buzz within ten minutes, my mind was set to a jumpy simmer.

I hadn't thought about a lot of things and people, my father and alcohol and anger, my mother and pain. Regardless of the buzz, I wouldn't let myself think about an abortion or even the fetus growing to term, or whatever the fate, the fragments of thoughts would attack quickly and randomly anyway.

I hadn't thought much about my best friend David. Ana was so much my friend in so little time that I hadn't felt the need. I was half-ass aware of my frustration, enough to know that I needed to seek out David for some guidance. He was the friend I always turned to.

David was going to be difficult to track down. Since he had been kicked out of high school for fighting, he was a vagabond, wandering couch to couch.

After I finished the wine, I went and grabbed some beer from the fridge. There were only a few left. I grabbed one and looked around in the liquor cabinet. I grabbed at the half-empty bottle of vodka, I had a quick second doubt and put it back.

After I finished the beer, I brushed my teeth again (without vomiting). I attempted to go upstairs to sleep.

"Sleep on the couch." Ana said.

"Really? I just brushed my teeth again."

"I can smell the wine from here. It's making me nauseous and I just got over being nauseous."

"Is there anything that doesn't make you nauseous?" I said.

She didn't answer.

I sulked back down the stairs, mumbling under my breath. I went back to the liquor cabinet and pulled out the bottle of vodka, fully intent on getting drunk. I had scruples enough to put the bottle back and lay down on the couch, I was angry but not angry enough to stay awake.

***

My brother woke me up, it was six in the morning.

"Don't you sleep?" I asked.

"I got my four, I'm good." He said.

Cy had this theory about sleep. He felt that four hours of sleep is perfectly fine for the human body, so long as the bedtimes and wake-ups are consistent. He tested his theory in prison and lives by it.

I sat up, he had a cup of coffee ready for me.

"Your girl already mad at you?"

"Yeah, I don't feel that I did anything wrong."

"Get used to it. That shit doesn't stop." He said. We went to the kitchen table.

My head wasn't clear enough to register anything fully, and a small headache was pulsing.

"I was thinking about what Ana had said about planting a garden. I think we should. Remember the gardens we had growing up? Dad had us rotate the surplus of survival seeds every year for the Victory Garden? I think it's a great idea. We can build terraces in the front and remove the sod from the other half of the backyard." Cy said.

"I'm getting paid soon, so I can get some seed from the farmer's market this weekend." I said.

"Don't worry about it, I got money. Money isn't a big deal. I want you to put your money into a savings account because as far as we know, we still have to live in this real world, not dad's world of ruin. I figured you could help me fix the place up. It's a dump. And we can renovate that whole attic so you don't have to feel like you're squatting. We can even put in walls around that toilet so it's not so prison-like." He said.

"I think Ana will be happy about the garden." I said.

"That's good, you guys are too new to be having problems already. But people raised like us will always have problems with vegans." He said.

"She's not even vegan. She's a fructarian. She doesn't eat harvested vegetables, only stuff that falls off naturally." I said.

"I've never heard of that." Cy said. "The new toilet should be here tomorrow. Buddy of mine is coming by with it. It's one of the pull chain models. It's actually from the seventies but it's never been used. Should be interesting. He said the only problem with it is that it's what they call 'Avocado Green'."

"So in other words, puke green."

***

"Do you write poetry Jacob?" Ana was kneeling and had a cigarette in one hand, a pen on paper on the window sill. The sun was bright and all over her face. The room was light dust and hard shadows. She wouldn't look at me. She blew smoke rings out of the window.

I was admiring her in the harsh light, this helped me from being angry with her. "I used to. Until I started to read all the crap I wrote. Silly stuff."

"Do you think emotions are silly?" She said.

I did think so, at that time, but couldn't say so. 'No' was all I said.

"You shouldn't be ashamed of how you feel." She blew more smoke out of the window. She was shining. "Poetry is a pithy way to express emotional outbursts."

"I thought you were done smoking?" I said.

"I am." She said and stubbed out the cigarette.

"I'm leaving to find my friend David."

"I know." She said.

I gave her a kiss on the cheek. She never turned her head.

Chapter 21: Fruitflies

I had to take three buses across town to find David. The last bus didn't have air conditioning, the less frequented routes always had the old worn-down buses. These types of buses always smell of piss and poverty, seats decorated in scribbled graffiti, relics of our time.

I was reading *Dr. Mantha's Compendium of Myth and Legend,* browsing the pages of Orpheus and the loss of his newly wedded wife to a snake in the grass.

Orpheus should have just jumped off a cliff in the first place. But the ever-depressed minstrel tried his hand at cheating death. The wonderful music he played on his lyre was not enough. It may have been enchanting enough to briefly make Tantalus forget about his hunger and thirst or to make the vulture eating Prometheus' liver do a double take and to pause Ixion's eternal wheel of torment. But his gift for music wasn't enough to dispel his own anxiety. He left his precious Eurydice in Hades due to his fear. The psychiatrists at FTC could have washed away his anxiety and grief with a lifetime supply of Freshax. Everything's alright with Freshax. Without it, he sadly wandered the world with the boon of the Gods while hypnotizing animals and teaching people the mysteries of the Universe. Until one day, some wine-drunken, sex-fiends took offense to his masterful music and celibacy and tore his ass apart spreading it throughout ancient Greece. His lesson was not learned. If you wander the world in sorrow after cheating death, you are not *living*.

Between paragraphs of reading, I looked at all the advertisements above the seats on the bus. There are always signs of food and pregnancy, and occasionally religious ones say NO to drinking/drugs and sex.

One clever religious ad read – Keep your hands together, Keep your legs together. There was a picture of a girl praying on her knees in a beam of light and below her also read – Pure-God-Love. Ad sponsored by Brand New Christ Church. In Dr. Mantha's myth book, Perseus was born this way, conceived as a golden shower.

There was an ad for the McMill's new EnergyMill Burger. A very slender female model with a disproportionally big smile filled with holy white teeth. For some reason, she was in a bikini in the center of the Cosmos surrounded by a colorful nebula. The ad read – **EnergyMill Burger is Everywhere Forever**. And below that was the McMill's bastard version of Einstein's equation which read – Eb=mc^2. This one was almost as bad as their commercials. The last one I saw was in the FTC. **EnergyMill Burger can neither be created nor destroyed. It can be eaten!** This was said by an Einstein-looking physicist looking into the Cosmos at the same bikini girl dancing with this enormous burger in the middle of a nebula.

Laws of the Universe do not apply in marketing.

But this was the more appropriate marketing campaign that replaced the original. People got offended when they likened the burger to an atom bomb – **It Will Blow You Away**. No need to really mention, but that campaign did not go over well in Japan.

But, nothing's sacred in capitalism.

Some others posted on the bus included:

A Buddhist monk eating the VeggieMill Burger on a mountain – **At One With The VeggieMill**.

An Aztec priest atop a ziggurat holding the SunMill Burger – **Eat Your Heart Out**.

The Aztec SunMill Burger advertisement was not translated into Spanish. It was no surprise that the SunMill campaign got disbanded. McMill's got away with everything and anything, even if it was just a short time. You could say they got away with murder, but that would not be a figure of speech. They had their dirty fingers in murderous regimes and drug cartels in the whole of Latin and South America.

A pregnant girl, about twelve or thirteen years old, huddled in a corner of an empty room – **Life Doesn't Hate You, It Awaits You. Call us.** There were others aimed at young pregnant girls in both English and Spanish.

I skipped the third bus and decided to walk the rest of the way.

David was not easy to track down. I had called everyone I knew to find a number to the house he was at. When I finally got it, it was the wrong number. This party house was the last place I knew David to be hanging out at. Some rich kid owned it, his eighteenth birthday gift from his parents. It was his first property which his parents intended for him to make money off of by renting it, a child's lesson in capitalism. No such luck. He went there for the good parties and always had a flock of suck-ups hovering like flies on shit. Needless to say, a lot of kids left their parents' houses to live there and try to keep up a perpetual party.

When I got there, the perpetual party had ended. The rich kid had apparently given up on paying a cleaning service. From the outside, the place should have been condemned. Beer cans and fast food wrappers and shriveled condoms where there wasn't weeds and tall grass, a few abandoned cars next to the garage and a possibly functioning one in the driveway. Someone must have tried to cut the lawn a few times, random bald patches.

I went to the front door. In black magic marker on the bottom of a pizza box, a sign read "Backdoor" with an arrow and an illustration of a lightbulb. The lightbulb had a smiling head with curly hair to the side and two disproportionate arms. Apparently it was an artist's rendition of the backside of a woman with a large bottom pulling up her pants up, beckoning everyone to the 'backdoor'. The crack of her ass was the lightbulb's filament.

I knocked at the backdoor for a while. I was getting ready to leave when the blinds cracked, a bunch of locks clattered.

David opened the door with a baking tin in his hand, fork sticking out of it, in his tighty-whitey underwear. He had magic marker writing all over himself, some were possibly tattoos he had gotten since I saw him last. There were words in Hebrew, the *actual* equation $E=mc^2$, some Cuneiform, a Greek phrase, the beginning of Shakespeare's intro to Hamlet's monologue – To Be or Not to be, and a fair amount of weird symbols and unrecognizable languages. There was a diagram of the Tree of Life from the Kabbalah, the book of Jewish Mysticism.

The house smelled like a garbage can that someone shit and pissed in after puking up a liquor store, the stench wafted out from behind him. David had 'X's drawn on his eyes, also. For anyone else, a surprise. But for me, the usual. He was having girl problems before I went to FTC which made his behavior even more erratic.

"Jake, James, Jacob, Yakov, friend. Wow. Good to see you." He would often call me by my Hebrew name and other ethnic versions of my name. He gave me an awkward hug.

David had what people would call a 'shit-eating grin'. Many people figured he was crazy, partly because of this. The other reason they thought him crazy was because of the random things he'd say that would make normal people feel awkward. He had never been to the FTC but had been to the poor people's version of it. When he was locked up, he never got to eat good food or talk with interesting psychologists or even meet attractive girls for that matter. The last of the government owned facilities weren't co-ed, and David always opted for solitary confinement.

"What's up man?" I said.

He was fidgeting with his fork in the baking tin.

"Come in, come in. This humblest of humble abodes." He said.

I walked in, waving my hands through a cloud of fruit flies. "What happen to this place?" I said.

"Shit happens." He gestured with his baking tin at the landfill interior. His laugh reminded me of a hyena, a madman's laughter. I was familiar with the laugh. Something was wrong.

"Hungry? Want some turkey loaf?"

He showed me what was in the baking tin, an over-dried and brown loaf of something, might have been a turkey long ago. It didn't even look edible. "No thanks." I didn't know what to say. I was awkward and I wasn't in my underwear.

"They cut off the power last week so I've been foraging for food. The gas is still on though. That's how I was able to disinfect this turkey loaf. It's kind of like jerky now. Jerky loaf." He said. He was laughing and stabbing at the loaf. "Now I have the place to myself. Mostly. Minus the few of us who are on a No Name basis. They come, they go. I haven't left. I'm waiting for a call from Natalie."

“Really? The phone’s still on? I thought it was turned off, but I actually got the wrong number.” I said.

“Yeah, but obviously King Herod has left his kingdom abandoned otherwise. No more maid service or grounds keeping or parties for that matter.” He said.

“Natalie? You’re still talking to her?”

“She was supposed to call me a week ago. Now I’m starting to worry. It’s making me lose sleep.” He said. “I’ve been up for days.” He pointed at his bloodshot eyes with his fork.

“You’re serious aren’t you?” I said.

“Enough about me. How was your little visit to the Felicity Treatment Center. Cakewalk, wasn’t it? Told you it would be. I mean, I’d take that any day instead of those shoddy county nuthouses.”

I took a moment to look around the place. It looked like a recycling center. There was trash everywhere, but it was highly organized into piles covered with flies. The dishes in the sink were also organized even though they were food encrusted. This was the work of David. He had Obsessive Compulsive Disorder, and like Ana, was also Bipolar.

David waved me to follow him. I bumped a bag of cans and puffed up a swarm of fruit flies. I fanned my face.

“Hey dude, they don’t bite.”

“I know. There are just so many.” I said.

“You get used to them, you know. I’ve even taken up studying them. Remember in science class? Spontaneous Generation?”

“Sure.”

“If I didn’t know any better, thanks to the late and great Louis Pasteur, I’d believe in Spontaneous Generation. Look here.” He showed me a bunch of random empty jars filled with fruitflies. “Their scientific name is *drosophila melanogaster.* In English, black-bellied lover of dew."

When I met David, he was obsessed with Louis Pasteur. I blamed Mr. Pasteur for David's germaphobia (a.ka. mysophobia). I probably knew more about Mr. Pasteur from David than any of my science classes.

David was always obsessed with someone or something at any given time. But he wasn't obsessed with Louis at that particular moment when I found him, just Natalie and the Kabbalah and fruitflies, Mr. Pasteur was a sidenote. He would eventually go on to compare Natalie to a fruit fly after I talked some sense into him that she wasn't going to call. 'That ungracious nymph. Blackhole-hearted lover of Nectar, that Whore for the Dew of the Gods.' He said.

David wasn't technically Jewish. He was home-raised with the Judaic faith by his mother, who wasn't technically Jewish. He never met his father, who was racially Jewish. His mother always told him that his father died in 'The War'. His mother taught him Hebrew and some traditions, but because of where we lived, he had no exposure to other Jewish people, in school or otherwise. Whenever David asked to go to a synagogue, his mother told him that there were none close to them, and she never drove so he took her word for everything.

It took him till puberty to find out the truth of what being matriarchal Jewish means.

At age thirteen, when he thought he would get his *bar mitzvah,* David learned, to his surprise, that he wasn't technically Jewish. His dreams of being the direct descendent of King David, and fighting in a modern holy war, were shattered along with his full belief in the Torah or the Old Testament. He would never bear the Shield of David again.

He converted briefly to Christianity, this was right before I met him, and even spend some time with the Quran. He would never lose his affinity to Judaism, or all Abrahamic religions for that matter, regardless of whatever personal beliefs he held.

He also lost faith in his mother, who finally decided to tell him the truth about everything. His dad hadn't died in 'The War', which was no 'war' in particular. He had always assumed there was some secret war in the holy lands of which his dad was a soldier of Yahweh. Not the case, his dad ditched his mother when he found out she was pregnant. She never looked for him. His dad never came back, never called. His birth certificate looked a lot like Ana's, mother's maiden name filled in and father's name blank.

His mother tried to explain that he could still be Jewish, that it's in the heart and that he could be a part of a reform synagogue. He would be accepted and have a place. But it was too late for David, he felt betrayed by his mother and father and faith.

At the time I met David, he was so disgusted with the Christianity that he would destroy anyone willing to argue with him, just like Ana. This was a fifteen year old who made thirty year old adults cry and quit and walk away, or occasionally threaten violence. And David was always one to accept violence with open arms so to speak.

So we stood in the pigsty that used to be a living room or a livable room. The only clean spot in the room was on the couch next to an ancient black phone where David was meant to sleep.

"You have to get out of this place, seriously." I said.

"I can't until Natalie calls."

"She isn't gonna call. You know it." I said. "Come stay at my brother's house with me and Ana."

David was silent for a while, he never answered me. He went around the house collecting pieces of paper he had written on.

"Where's the bathroom?" I asked.

He pointed down the hallway. I shouldn't have asked, should've held it in.

"Use the sink." He yelled after me. "If you have to shit, go outside behind the shed."

***

There is a prank that teenager's play which consists of covering a toilet bowl with plastic wrap. This is done with great care, the plastic has to be perfectly spread with no ripples or wrinkles so that the victim cannot detect the prank. The intention is that the victim lets loose excrement but instead of relief, a nasty mess, on and around the toilet and the victim's buttocks.

When I walked into that bathroom, I had an instant gag reflex. Like a horrible murder scene, where does one start to look?

The toilet was the star of the show, the murder victim. It was full to the brim with a foul swirl of different shades of shit and covered with plastic wrap. I had assumed the wrap was on there not as a prank but a way to stifle the stench or a preventive measure. With further investigation, someone fell for the unintentional prank, several times. I couldn't bring myself to even go in there.

There was a time that I had contemplated puking in an outhouse when I was camping. This is such a paradox, when you can't puke because something is that disgusting. That bathroom looked like the inside of a pit-toilet, the walls were splattered browns and speckled greens, dried blood and shit on concrete modern art. IRA political prisoners painted such art in their cells during the Dirty Protest.

David started telling me the genesis of the bathroom's demise, but he stopped himself. "Not that important, I think."

David was dressed and ready to go, had a bag packed. He had managed to get most of the marker off of his face. He carried a book under his arm, the Kabbalah. He always carried a book. Well before I met him, it was the Torah. Shortly before I met him, it was the Bible then the Quran then the Dhammapada.

"Someone should burn this place down." He said.

We left.

***

While I was away, Ana was busy as usual. She decorated our attic room with what she called *Thinspiration*. And her mood was completely opposite of when I left. I understood Bipolar Disorder. She hugged and kissed me. "Oh, come see." She said. I left David downstairs.

"Most anorexic girls I know hang up waif models for *Thinspiration*. I used to do it too, but now this is my *Thinspiration* for my 'Revolution'."Ana said.

There were two decorated walls. One was covered with images of historical figures, there were only three that I recognized, Mahatma Gandhi, St. Catherine of Sienna (the same icon as Ana's tattoo on her torso). She explained them all to me. They were all *hungerstrikers* (as she called them).

She stood at the historical people wall like a teacher. I sat on the bed, the avid student.

There was a black and white photo of Marion Dunlop who was a suffragette and a hunger striker. Her revolution was for the rights of women. Many of her fellow revolutionaries died as a result of force-feeding.

"Do you know how they force-fed the suffragettes?" Ana asked. "They would shove a tube down their throats down to here." She tapped on her sternum then pointed at an old poster under the portrait of Marion Dunlop. There were three men holding a woman down and shoving a beer-bong down her throat. "They would pour a mixture of milk and eggs. Horrid!"

The photo of Gandhi was largest, he was sitting cross-legged with a *charakha,* or Indian spinning wheel, making his homespun yarn. Again with the British. That Empire had its greedy little fingers in everything. The apple doesn't fall far from the tree, America's got those same relentless fingers.

"And you should know this guy." She pointed at Cesar Chavez holding a bullhorn. I didn't recognize who he was by the picture, I had only seen him on a political mural which was painted in a very childish style. Cesar Chavez fought for the rights of agricultural workers and Latino civil rights. "This American Hell can use a revolutionary like him again." Ana would have made a great teacher.

"I'll tell you some more about St. Catherine of Sienna."

I nodded.

"St. Catherine learned the power of the hunger strike from her sister. Her sister starved herself until her husband would stop mistreating her. Then she abruptly died in childbirth, and Catherine was expected to marry the widower. She originally agreed to her parent's wishes of marriage and got prettied up and even went as far as dying her hair.

But she could not go through with it. Her love for Jesus was much too strong. So she cut off her hair. To further defy her father, she fasted until her father gave into her wishes.

Not only was starvation a way to defend herself from male dominance, but it was a very spiritual thing. Because of these qualities, she has been one of my biggest inspirations. And I'm not even fond of Christianity, but I appreciate many of its values. It's just too bad most of its followers don't, they are mostly hypocrites and destroyers."

"She became a very influential person throughout the church, and was always fasting. She became ill with eating, I know this feeling. Her nourishment was with God, and mine is with my Goddess, it's all the same, the Universe is genderless. During the fast she had in defiance of her father, she went into a room inside her head and would eventually find comfort and peace. The hunger no longer pained her. She never suffered from hunger again. Amazing woman, and this was in the 14th century." She said.

On the opposite wall was a collage quite different from the one filled with iconic faces of important figures. The wall was filled with death and starvation. I moved closer to see details. There were several pictures of starving people (though mostly children) of all races and pictures of slaughterhouse scenes, interwoven with those were haughty pictures of rich white men in suits. There were African children huddled on the ground in one and a literal handful of others outstretching their stick arms for some morsels, skin and bones and bulbous heads. There were holocaust victims standing naked in showers, skeletons with faces. Stick people and wealthy happy people laughing and drinking next to factories filled with cattle carcasses hanging from hooks next to beakless chickens.

"My friend David is downstairs. You want to meet him?" I said.

***

"Are you a meat-eater too?" Ana said.

"Well, I try not to eat the ass-half of the cow, out of respect for my friend Jacob here." David said.

Ana didn't laugh. David cackled. "But lately I'll eat anything for I've barely had enough to get by in the last month." David the Hyena.

"Do you have an eating disorder too then?"

"Heavens no, I'm simply very poor."

"There is nothing wrong with that. That's the simplest form of revolution. To be so poor that you can't buy anything. Nothing wrong with that." Ana said.

Chapter 22: Food For Thought

We three were going down to the river. I had a bag full of clay in one hand, Ana's hand in the other. She had her hand-woven grass backpack on that was filled with different things she planned on doing. David talked to us the whole way there, mainly about Natalie and what a conniving and lying succubus she was.

There were gravid clouds rumbling in the distance and the air was warm, not hot. No one cared.

We were at our usual spot. Ana was watching me start the fire. I was striking a small piece of flint with a rusty hunk of metal I had found. Ana had built the bird's nest tinder-bundle so well that it had caught spark with ease. Then David and I made a few bowls and cups while Ana was basket weaving.

"I think I'll make an axe." I said to David.

David was kneading a hunk of clay on a rock. "I think I'll make me a sling." He said.

"I'm not surprised." I said.

"But don't worry Ana. It'll only be used for giant Philistines, not for innocent creatures." David said.

Ana snickered then looked at me. "What do you need an ax for Jacob?"

"To make stuff out of wood." I said.

"Not living trees?" She said.

"Of course not." I said. I knew to not get Ana started about trees.

David struck up a conversation with Ana. I looked around for a large rock suitable for making an ax or hammer.

I was happy that Ana had taken to my friend and Cy and vice versa. Cy and David were the closest people in my life before her, so I couldn't help but be concerned about them getting along. Ana was so completely devoted to her morals that I had feared anything against them could make her angry and mean. And David was not one to care about anything that left his mouth at any given time. I had told him all about Ana on the bus ride back, so he had fair warning, but David was always unpredictable with the things he'd say.

"There must be something to say about thirst and dehydration." I said. The fire was lit. Ana was seated, unloading her grass backpack. David was off in some reeds, collecting.

"What's that?"

"I don't think a *dehydration strike* exists. Or even worse, a *suffocation strike.* It's just not enough time to make anyone think about it." I said.

"Are you mocking me?" Ana said.

"Not at all." I said. "I was just thinking." I crept back into my shell.

David was making snake coils, we all knew the same basic pottery skills from art class. We'll all know how to live in this world. His coils were perfect unlike mine. He hurried to finish, he sensed the tension between me and Ana. David tried diverting Ana's attention through conversation.

"Jacob, I'm really sorry if I'm so irritable. I can't help it. I've been catching myself and restraining the best I can. I hope you understand what I'm dealing with, because I can feel you pulling away from me. And now that you have a friend around, it'll be easier for you to detach yourself."

“I’m not pulling away. I just want things to be okay. I don’t want to fight about anything.”

“You seem like you don’t want to deal with it.” She said.

I bit my tongue, figuratively and my lip, literally.

“I want for you to be okay, and me to be okay, and us to be okay.” I said. I thought of the book *I’m Okay You’re Okay,* and I was self-conscious to how stupid my words sounded.

“Nothing’s okay Jacob.”

“I know. Everything’s fucked! You’re thinking about abortion no matter what I have to say about it, and it doesn’t matter much because meanwhile you’re starving yourself to death. And what am I suppose to do?” I yelled this. I inherited this awful family trait from my father who got it from his father and so on. My brother called it ‘going from zero to sixty’. He had inherited it too.

I got up and left her there next to the fire.

“Don’t walk away from me!” She said. Her tone was fierce.

Now I was angry, blood trickled from inside my lip, I refused to look back. I was starving, the coppery taste triggered a carnivorous savagery. I went looking for David.

My father had taught me how to flintknap stone tools, axes, knives, and spearheads. The area we lived in didn’t provide much in the way of naturally knappable stone so we had to heat treat certain rocks or buy chert and obsidian from rock shops. I also learned to make tools with the bottom of glass bottles which were in more abundance than knappable stones along the river. Certain flat bottom bottles were nice for making arrowheads or small knives. Glass can be just as dangerous as obsidian to work with, and I had scars on my hand to prove this. This was after several years of working with gloves until I was comfortable, and of course until my dad started calling me a pussy.

I found a brown bottle of St. Agni that used to hold forty ounces of 'Premium Malt Liquor'. Agni was the Hindu deity of fire and apparently the patron saint of pungent malt liquor. St. Agni was a favorite of my group of friends when we were twelve years old. A forty-ounce bottle of malt liquor can really get a twelve year old drunk.

David was sitting under a bridge when I found him, slinging rocks at the foundation. He had braided a sling out of the strands of rope that used to be his belt. His shirt was off and tied around his head like an Egyptian pyramid worker or Jewish slave (he would prefer). He didn't wash off all the writing that was there, some of it wasn't even attempted. $E=mc^2$ and some others were tattoos, not magic marker.

"Are you hungry?" I said.

"Of course I am, look at me." He laughed. His rib cage looked like a xylophone.

"Let's go hunting."

"Ana won't stand for that. What are you going to tell her?"

"She doesn't have to know and I don't care right now. I'll eat whatever I want to, no matter what she says. For now I'll make a new fire then I'll run back to the house and get us some booze. I feel like drinking tonight."

"Drinking?" David laughed. "That's fine, but what do you plan on hunting? There are only squirrels around right now and raccoons and opossums tonight."

"I'll eat anything right now, it doesn't matter. Opossum doesn't sound very appealing though."

“I’d rather have squirrel, honestly.” David said. “Have you ever used a sling?”

“No, I haven’t.” I said.

“It’s hard. I’ve been practicing for a while now, and I can barely hit anything.” He said. “The pouch was the hardest thing to make. It has to hold the rock well enough to spin fast.”

“The squirrels down here aren’t even afraid of anyone.” I said.

I struck the glass with a rock for a basic shape while David kept practicing slinging rocks at the wall structure of the bridge. Using my metal striker firestarter, I flaked off bits of the glass to make an edge. This three inch knife blade had endless uses such as shaving, skinning, carving, et cetera. Our purpose was skinning.

I left David practicing under the bridge and walked slowly back to our camp. Ana was gone. The fire was snuffed out. The cups and bowls were still there, drying in the half-showing sun. I put them into my survival bag and carried them back to my brother’s house. I was expecting to see Ana and half-hoping to resolve our little conflict before I went back to the river, no such luck. She wasn’t in the house, not in our room, not in the living room, or the bathroom. That’s as far as I looked. I checked the liquor cabinet, plenty to choose from. I picked the fullest and biggest bottles, they happened to be Gin and Brandy. I didn’t like Gin, but I didn’t care. I just wanted to be drunk and to forget about Ana and the fetus for awhile.

***

Down by the river in the city, every rare once in awhile, you run across a fox or coyote or a deer. Every now and again, you might see a hawk or eagle, even rarer an owl. But these creatures always remained elusive regardless of the little harm that came to them. Squirrels and raccoons on the other hand let you get within feet of them. They dug through your empty fast food wrappers right in front of you.

By the time I got back to the bridge, David was standing next to a dead fox, staring down at it sling swaying in hand.

"Not exactly a dirty Philistine." He said. He was somber and didn't look up at me. "I've never killed an animal before. I mean, with my own hands at least." He was on the verge of tears.

"We have to hurry and get his guts out. It's warm out. How long has he been dead?" I said. I wanted to console him in some way, but I never had consolation when I killed my first animal. I figured he had to deal with those thoughts himself.

My first kill was a squirrel, I shot it with a .22 caliber rifle from ten feet away. I was twelve and didn't think much of the killing since my dad had hunted since I could remember. I didn't realize the gravity of taking life until my dad made me gut and skin that squirrel.

I was between being scared and nervous, not sure exactly what I felt, except I knew I didn't want to deal with the poor thing's little body. 'You killed it, you skin it, and you eat it.' My dad told me what to do as I did it. This consisted of him barking an order then correcting what I was doing by saying something like, 'The thing's not going to bite now, is it? Now stop being such a pussy. You'll never survive Apocalypse if you can't deal with a little blood.' When I was finished cooking and eating the squirrel, my dad told me that I was a man now, that I had just passed my puberty rite. I was still a boy, still felt like a boy under that bridge with David and the Fox. I felt like a boy when I met Ana. Much of me is still a boy. We're all cleverly disguised children.

I didn't want to put David through the same thing I went through, and I wasn't his father so I wasn't comfortable with barking any kind of orders at him. I showed him how.

'Let's string him up right under the bridge, so no one sees us.' I said. I picked up the fox by the hind legs. I could see it was a female. "It's a girl."

"We have to name her first." David said. He was very serious, he'd held back crying with a comfortable laugh. David hadn't cried since he learned about his father.

"Do whatever you want, but we've got to get these guts out." I said. "And we need to start another fire. We'll be eating soon."

"I want to help." David said. "I think I'll name her Felicitas, after the Roman Goddess of Luck or the saint from Rome. St. Felicitas watched her seven sons die because she didn't denounce Christ. Now that is faith."

"Is there anything left of that rope?" I asked. I gave David the bottle of gin. "Have a swallow, it'll help you not think so much in the meantime."

My first lesson with alcohol was this same thing. My dad stopped me from skinning and told me to swig from this pint of whiskey. I spit it out, choking. 'Just drink it! It'll help you not think about it so much.' By the time I was sixteen, it became a ritual to be half drunk when skinning bigger animals like deer. Over those years of hunting with my dad, it was normal to me. He had once got drunk enough to admit to me that he still had to drink to deal with *killing*. He was a Vietnam vet.

I strung Felicitas up by her hind legs on the bolts that stuck out of the concrete slabs directly under the bridge's base. These slabs of concrete were decorated in graffiti and strewn with the personal effects of homeless people who were all absent in search of handouts for booze.

The little glass knife I made was small and razor sharp, it was hard to hold without cutting my hand. David ripped off some leather so I could make a small handle.

I started gutting her, belly first.

David stepped in and helped. His face looked discolored for a slight moment, and I expected him to barf all over, but he kept it in and pulled out the intestines.

I did the rest, organ by organ. I handed him the heart.

"You might want to eat the heart and set its spirit free." I said.

He took a bite out of the fox's heart and handed back to me. I was kidding, David was not.

"No thanks." I took another swig of gin.

Once David caught on to what I was doing, he took over and did the rest.

"A lot of people remove the head, but my dad thinks that's because they don't want to deal with the fact that they killed something similar to them, kind of like when people in cannibal situations have to put the face down and away." I said. "I think that it's more trouble than it's worth." I pulled down the carcass and took a few large swigs out of the bottle of brandy. I slung the carcass on my shoulders and wiped finger-lines of blood across my cheeks and chest. David draped the fox-skin over his shoulder.

The guts and rest of the vitals were left by some bum's pillow underneath the bridge.

***

We sat by the fire, drunk already. The fox carcass was on a makeshift spit, meat searing and overcoming the fresh death smell with the tantalizing smokiness of cooking flesh.

The sun was behind the tree line, sky was pink and baby blue. The fire licked Felicitas, our sacred dinner, David's first kill, and my gesture of defiance towards Ana and all she loved. Also, this act was the essence of my own revolution towards this weak and incapable society of self-worshiping idiots.

I looked over the fire at David sitting on a rock. There were so many types of writing that I couldn't even recognize. One in particular looked like Arabic.

"What's that one say?" I asked.

"Which one?" He didn't look up.

"The Arabic looking one."

He laughed. "That's Aramaic in the Syriac script. It's the only Aramaic that still exists in the Bible. It says 'Oh God, why have you forsaken me?" He said it out loud in Aramaic also. "I'll never forget it."

"Does your mom know that you've been getting tattoos?" I said.

"She knows and she is horrified. I told her that it's no big deal, because if she is worried about my body at the Day of Judgment, she can have a rabbi remove them. But of course, God will have to get over the fact that I was enwombed and born from a gentile woman." He said.

David also had tattoos of the prisoner numbers of both of his grandfathers from World War II. These were his first two tattoos that he did himself with a needle wrapped in thread and some India ink. His mother's father was Roma Gypsy and had a number (his mother's mother was Armenian and didn't have a number but she did survive genocide). His father's parents, both Jewish survivors at Dachau, had numbers, but David found it impossible to contact anyone in that family to get the actual numbers. Everyone hung up on him when he asked them (David didn't like small talk). He made one up that correlated with the Nazi's number system at Dachau.

David took a big pull off the gin bottle and passed it to me. "Do you remember the time when I found out that I wasn't truly Jewish?"

I nodded and took a drink and turned the fox carcass on the spit.

"Well, I figured I had no choice but to turn to Christianity at the time, and when I got to the part in the gospel where Jesus is crucified, he said that, right before he died, and I couldn't help but feel like that, to feel forsaken by my father and shunned by my own people under their God. Race and religion, it's all a joke. Different gods with different names and rules, they're all as petty as the people that made them in the first place."

I took another swallow of brandy and checked if the meat was done. "She's done."

We drank and ate the flesh of Felicitas. I told him about Kronos eating his children and spitting out the rock that was supposed to be Zeus which became the Navel of the World.

I pulled *Dr. Mantha's Compendium of Myth and Legend* out of my survival rucksack.

"*Omphaloskepsis*. That's the word I was thinking of. When I read this, I felt like this is what I am. An *omphaloskeptic,* or a 'navel-gazer'. Dr. Mantha describes *omphaloskepsis* as being 'a passionate self-fulfilling state of an individual's will i.e. egotistical meditation per se. This is me, this is wrestling to me. Even with the way I feel about Ana, I will not stop wrestling. And I won't stop being ready for this world to collapse. I can't help it." I said.

I picked some more fox flesh. The crispy strips of fox flesh tasted fine, especially against the background of the taste of brandy. All we were missing was the wild garlic and dandelion greens salad that we ate earlier when Ana was around.

"You know I don't believe in Jesus the way these people do. I feel that I am Jesus at times. And this world doesn't even know what to do with me." David grabbed the bottle of gin and pulled the fox fur from his shoulder. "I could shout in their faces 'Hey you, assholes! The world is ending now, I'm ending it, right now, come hither, let me take you away from this living hell! Do you even care? Do you even want to come with me to the promised land?' I could be this mythical Jesus with a real heaven to take them to and no one would go, no one would care.

You know Jacob, they all think we're crazy. And they're right, we are. And the world has always been ending, we just happen to exist in the sickest and ugliest version of it yet. And no one truly knows when it's finished. And who would care anyway? Unless you slice your wrists or put a rope around your neck or jump in front of a train or shoot yourself in the face, nobody knows shit about the end. But *those* people know. We know that deep down inside our world is a sick joke, if we chose to see it that way. If I shout at those kinds of people, they'll laugh and say 'Yeah so, what's the big deal?' and they would be right. What is the big deal?"

David was standing there with his arms spread wide as if nailed to a crucifix, Felicitas' fur in one hand and the bottle in the other. "And girls don't like nice guys, what does that even mean? I gave myself to that woman, and she took off, like a nymph. Clever and supple sodomite nymph."

"Forget about her. She was nothing but problems anyway." My words were slurring.

"Jacob."

"Yeah?"

"You've got a girl who really loves you. You need to realize that."

We went on for a few more hours into the night, stumbling for more firewood and drinking straight booze with no reservation.

I was wobbling next to the fire while David watched me. The fire was a thousand flames and the skeletal remains of Felicitas remained over it, charring like the night.

David asked me questions about the baby, even being drunk and mildly cathartic with my emotions, I said nothing to him about it.

That was one of my last memories that night. David wrote down his version of what happened after.

***

I woke up on the couch, my head pounding, the sun blasting through the window around a slight silhouette. Ana was standing there, facing either me or the sun. I covered my face with my arm.

There was a gallon of water, a bottle of aspirin, and a couple of candy looking wafers. This was my brother's 'care package', as he called it. The wafers were glucose tablets which he said helped stabilize the liver's metabolism. He was a professional drinker, otherwise known as a functional addict. I popped some aspirin and chugged down near half the gallon of water.

I still couldn't tell if Ana was facing me or not. I lay back down and chewed on one of the tablets, breathing heavy.

"Did you have a good time?" Ana said.

It took me a minute to speak, my throat was paralyzed. “I don’t remember.”

“Do you remember what you said to me when you got home last night?”

“No. Where did you go after you left the river? I came back here after you left and you were gone.” I said. I sat up. My face itched with dried blood of the fox.

“Look at you. *You’re* a murderer, just like the rest.” She said, short of screaming.

“I didn’t kill it.”

“Doesn’t matter.” She said.

“Where’d you go?” I said.

“Doesn’t matter.” She said and we sat in silence for eternal minutes. “I forgive you though. We all murder something at some point right?”

“I guess so.” I couldn’t attach thoughts very well, my head was still an anvil.

“A monster lurks in all of us. We hide this beast most of the time, some better than others. We hate this thing that allows us to perform horrors on everything, ourselves and those close to us, our children and our parents, our animals and our plants, our planet. We devour everything. None of us lacks this monster I’ve come realize. Even me. I try so hard to not let myself do anything that I deem horrible, but my thoughts and feelings come to a contradiction, and this is where this ruthless beast lives in me.”

“I had an abortion three years ago. I never told you. I’m embarrassed. But I’m mostly embarrassed because I was completely fine with what I had done after a few days. I told myself over and over that this embryo or zygote death was simply an act of being spared from this mockery of true Life. And I believed this for those three years until now. Now, with you, I don't know what to think anymore. And my convictions are stronger than ever. I'm slowly getting rid of all my hypocrisies."

At that, she threw a braided lock of her hair at me, it hit my chest. She turned fully around to face me. She was more than a silhouette and I could make out her face. She had cut all her hair off.

"You're right about a lot of things Jacob. The hair-dying and makeup and overzealous grooming habits are contradictory to my revolution." She was referring to a moment of my defiance to her when I had told her that make-up was silly and she didn't need it. What I actually said was far less eloquent than what she had just said. She admitted that it was a remnant of her low self-esteem which she wanted to do away with. Her mask. She listed a few of her goals, things she needed to work on, habits she needed to break.

"I've got to go and work at Demos. Are you coming by to get me after you get off of work?"

"Yeah, of course, if you want me to." I said.

She came over to me and kissed me on top of my head. I was shocked she got that close to me, with fox blood all over my face.

"And I'm not getting rid of *it!"*

***

Before I took a shower, I stared at myself in the long mirror hanging on the door. Some of the blood had wept off my face. It triggered a clip of memory of me running in the rain from the river. I remembered yelling about 'talking to God' and 'talking to myself'. I had a drunken moment years before when I ditched my religion. I had figured that my religion was nothing more than me being schizophrenic, that I talked to God only to realize that I had been listening and talking to myself.

In the mirror with the shower running, I told myself. 'The Gods are inside us.'

I had dismissed the pouch of fat developing around my waist. I could still see my ribs and abdominal muscles, so I felt good about my weight.

But I felt blurry.

In the shower I kept switching the water from the hottest to the coldest, shocking my body. It reminded me of the Roman's and their bathhouses. Besides crucifying and puking, the Roman's knew how to bathe therapeutically. Scandinavian's and Russian's still use saunas for heat therapy. And that was exactly what I needed, therapy. I thought about trying to reach Dr. Pavlovich but dismissed it. There are too many kids in the world with greater problems than my own.

David was sitting at the kitchen table when I came out of the bathroom. He had a small stack of newspaper pages, he was reading one of them. It wasn't the news he was reading but the letters superimposed on it, written in black magic marker in his handwriting, like some of the words written on his body.

"How much of last night do you remember?" David said.

"Not very much." I said.

"I wrote a story of the scene under the bridge when the storm hit. You were very drunk and inspired. So I took the liberty of writing a story about it."

"Were did you stay last night?" I said. I looked at the papers, trying to decipher what was written.

"I stayed down there with the bums. They didn't have anything interesting to add, but the situation felt right. I have a problem sleeping anyway so I figured I'd stay up until you had to go to work." David said.

"You can stay here, my brother won't mind." I said.

"Read this when you get a chance. I'll probably take a nap and go wander a bit. I won't be around tonight, you and your woman need some alone time."

He rolled the papers up into a scroll and put a thick rubber-band around it.

"Take this with you, read it on your break. It looks longer than it is."

***

I was doing the little routine of scraping the leftover food into the Sinkerator and setting up racks of dirty dishes to go through the Auto-Washer 300 when Chef Jeff approached me about a trick of his.

He told me that working in a restaurant was the best way to get free food. He called himself a *freegan* which meant that he didn't purchase any animal products, but he allowed himself to eat anything that will be thrown out. In our case, we were disposing fifty dollar plates of food.

"People barely eat some of this stuff." He was standing next to me at the washing station, pulling in plates from the busboy through the busing window.

"Lookee here. What is this? Today's special. Two forkfuls out of it. Instead of scraping this awesome morsel of food down the abyss, just shove it in your mouth and continue working." He did just that. He grabbed the chunk with his hand and stuffed it in his mouth. He pulled the next plate, it was half of an appetizer, and handed it to me. He told me to 'go ahead' through his mouthful of food.

Before he went back to his station he said, "you're going to have to be freegan if you want to last with Ana. You probably learned the hard way about bringing animal products into a place she stays."

I nodded and smiled, but I really wanted to punch him in the face. He had to have been with Ana to know so much. I changed my focus back to the food.

I stuffed my face. I spent the first few times only eating off the plates of food that were eaten out of the least, but then I had to stop myself, because I did not discriminate. I could easily eat everything that was coming through the busing window. And I did, for awhile.

When my belly was protruding and I was feeling encumbered, I went and relieved my stomach of its contents in our workers' bathroom. I had never filled a toilet that much before.

I was in this awkward kind of heaven with this strange ever-flowing cornucopia that the Gods eat from. This was Zeus' horn-of-plenty taken from the she-goat Almathea who suckled him.

This endless supply of half-touched food was the kind of bliss when you do what you want and don't have any guilt for what was being done, but regardless you still have to hide what you're doing from God or Gods or whoever. On the contrary of feeling guilt, I felt I was doing the opposite. I was no longer that wasteful bulimic that Ana so despised, I was being revolutionary in my own special way. I was a walking and talking garbage disposal. With doing exactly what the Sinkerator does, I was getting some enjoyment out of my job. I didn't feel *alienated* like Chef Jeff. But then again, all of my waste, my shit and piss and puke would be mixed with oil and transformed into fertilizer for the genetically modified crops of Santomon.

On my lunch break, I had no desire to order my free meal, so I went and read David's story of me being drunk around a fire under a bridge with some bums.

Jacob.

He who wrestles with God.

He who wrestles with himself.

He who climbs up and climbs down.

Lo, he stands by the fire, the Usurper's anger, the Foreseer's gift to men.

The flame of creation and destruction.

The womb of civilization. The tomb.

Hobbling men congregate round the light of Jacob's fire. "Can we stay, can we stay?" They say.

"What have you done you trolls?" Jacob screams at the gathering hoard, the womanless avatars of Mankind under the Evolution Bridge. "Nothing. You've done nothing! You mimic the torture of Prometheus and now you ask for fire. You willingly take the vulture to your own livers with your Dionysus' crisis. You forsook your gift and ask for it again. I will teach you. You will learn again."

Jacob grabs a stick and plank of wood. Next to his fire he starts another with a spinning axis on dry tinder.

He breathes out. "Fiat Lux."

A beastly man offers blessing from God while approaching Jacob. "May He bless you!"

"He? He? Who? Do you mean me? God is inside me, and inside you. I talk to God, you talk to God. But God talks to no one. God does not talk. Your petty words and blessings and prayers do nothing but belittle the Unknowable Cosmic Concept, and you call that 'He' and make it 'Speak'. Fools! I will take back the gift of fire lest you change your ways." Jacob says.

Jacob holds the elixir of the gods above the fire and pours. The fire erupts. Tongues of flame lick the void.

"Eat you fools. May your cornucopia be always full so you can set your fire to this world. You apes living like rats in the endless trash so that someday you'll become men. Men that live in this world." Jacob commands the trolls to the carcass.

They eat not of it.

They drink only from his bottle.

***

After I got off of work, I went to pick up Ana from the Demos Book Co-Op. The store front was closed, but people were always working throughout the night. The people who ran the co-op were so laid-back that most of the volunteers never even felt like they were working. I had helped Ana a number of times and never felt burdened by the task at hand. There is nothing burdensome in the work of a good cause, and in a modern society, making books affordable and accessible to people that appreciate them, is a good cause.

Chef Jeff called it *alienation.* 'When you get exploited for your labor, that empty feeling you get, that's alienation.'

On the walk there, I became conscious of my pouch of fat under my belly button. It had been weeks since I cared. It was still a pinch. Nothing I couldn't lose after some regular physical conditioning. I had felt that I needed more of the non-purging bulimia in my regimen.

The summer nights of River Heights buzzed with everything gone wrong in the world. Angry couples drunk and screaming at each other, kids getting lashed for whatever their strung-out parent thought they did wrong, dog-fights in the garages, overdosed teenagers dead between some buildings, prostitutes getting straightened by their masters inside of luxury sedans, and the city glistened with the gems of artificial light, our surrogate stars.

Ana had looked up at me when I came into the warehouse part of Demos. She was stamping a logo on the inside cover of books and writing them down on a list. I just watched her, admiring. Before arriving, I was worried that I wouldn't think of her the same without her hair, but on the contrary, it made me love her more. Her defiance was always a given, but the fact that she could disregard her insecurities in one simple act, enamored me more than I had been.

For as beautiful as she looked to me, I was also paradoxically afraid. Her hair disguised how thin her face actually was. Her cheek bones were so sharp and her nose had a deeper cleft in it. It could have been the drastic lighting of the warehouse, but something wasn't right to me. But as with most things wrong in my life, I just pretended like everything was okay.

"How are you feeling?" She asked me.

"Better, much better. Did you want some help?" I said.

"Sure, if you want to. I need the stacks of boxes over there moved."

"Okay. I want to say that I'm sorry."

"I know. And thank you." She said. "I made you a book list. Before we leave, take a look at it, and I'll get whatever one you want to read first."

After finishing whatever tasks I could help with, I perused a pile of miscellaneous magazines. In one of these stacks was a copy of *Psychology Now* with Dr. Pavlovich on the cover. The title on the side read 'Radical Treatment: Wisdom of the Ancients'.

"Look!" I showed Ana what I had found. I was excited like a little kid.

"Oh, wow. What was he doing at FTC? I knew he was a good shrink. He was the one that opted for three of my releases, that's why they didn't have him counsel me this last time. He always defended me, and those assholes at FTC would have had me committed the minute I turned eighteen." She said.

"He gave me *Dr. Mantha's Compendium of Myth and Legend.*"

I sat there while Ana finished up and read the article.

***

It was an interview with Dr. Pavlovich about his radical views of psychology. There was a picture of him standing in a cemetery next to an open grave. He held a skull in his palm, it was a mild parody of Hamlet holding poor Yorick's skull, the realization of the joke of death. Yorick was Hamlet's childhood jester.

That night, Ana had me read the monologue and added Hamlet to my booklist. She told me that the picture of Dr. Pavlovich was amusing in such a reference to psychology, because there is this notion of Hamlet's madness which is debatable. He went to such great lengths to plan his own demise, let alone the culprits in his father's death. Ana thought that the reference may have been a loose connection to Dr. Pavlovich's publicly criticized support for Dr. Kevorkian who battled with the government over laws on suicide.

But then again, Dr. Povlovich was criticized for everything, and vice versa.

***

Psychology Now Interviewer: Dr. Pavlovich, it's my pleasure to meet with you today.

Dr. Pavlovich: Thank you for having me.

PN: It's hard to know where to start with you. You have been very progressive in modern psychology by way of ancient philosophy, and for that you have been fiercely criticized by your peers. Lately you have been promoting a type of new psychological technique. Can you tell us about it?

Dr P: Yes, I'd love to. I like to refer to the age-old proverb, 'Give a man a fish, feed him for a day. Teach a man to fish, feed him for a lifetime.' I've been trying to relate this to therapy. I feel that humans are capable of most anything and everything, so why not give people the tools they need to repair their own minds. If you think of the relationship of life and the human mind, it's a constant journey of despair and comfort, *ups* and *downs* so to speak. And it's in psychology that we deal with repairing the damage that's done through this process. The problem I have with some modern psychology is the restriction of psychological knowledge with a patient. I am only judging this by my own personal methods when I was younger. What I've been working on lately is how to relate psychology directly to the patient, in his or her own personal interests to the point that they'll never need me again. I've been digging into the history of humans as far back as we know. And what we know about the human mind twenty-thousand years ago is that his psychology was directly related to his or her externalized religious experience. Freud and Jung were right in relating all of these psychological ideas to mythology and religion, and because of this connection we can relate psychology to the religious experience in a secular manner. The method I'm trying to develop is working with an individual with whatever they are interested in. If someone likes Eastern religions, I'll introduce some Taoist or Buddhist or Hindu teachings in a non-religious way, and if the patient chooses to take with them a religious experience, so be it. This goes for the Bible, Torah, and Quran also. The Abahamic religions also have relative concepts to repairing the mind. Many religious people have criticized this, they think I'm exploiting their belief systems, using it as a tool out of religious context. That isn't the case though, you can ask any Christian or Muslim I have helped. I'm using their own personal doctrine to help them psychologically learn to help themselves. And if the patient is atheist or agnostic, then they have that choice to look upon these ancient texts as repairing tools. I do not represent the religion, that is what makes the process secular. My ultimate goal is to have a person learn ways to deal with themselves psychologically and emotionally in any helpful ways available. The hope is that the person will never have to see a shrink again.

PN: Some psychologists have criticized you for trying to debunk the whole science of psychology. How do you feel about that?

Dr. P: I think they should criticize me endlessly as long as it's in the realm of science and not at my person as many do. Reviewing and refuting my methods is the spirit of the scientific method. We can't reach an understanding of the Truth if we don't constantly question reality. What I think some of them are really trying to sabotage is their livelihood, which I am not. I'm sure that they'll still have enough patients to keep them in the six figures to pay for their luxury. I am proposing a method that undermines the profit in perpetual treatment, and some don't like that. The thought that this harms the psychologists' business is silly because our society is so large and psychologically at-risk due to the nature of large civilizations and modernity. There is an endless line of patients who need help.

PN: The pharmaceutical companies have been on a warpath against you and your colleagues also. What are your thoughts on this?

Dr. P: This is the main issue, and it all stems from money and power. It is much deeper and viler than the issue some psychologists have regarding money alone. Our hyperactive capitalism does not have a finish line to achieve, it's constantly eating itself to grow. There can never be enough money to make. Pharmaceutical companies are the paradigm of the unrestrained capitalist enterprise, they know no bounds. The madness of greed is manifold that has no end, unless someone or some governing body stops and limits them. They are now clearing the way to give small children psychotropic drugs. When and where does it stop, it's awful. They want people to be sick, mentally and physically and spiritually. That is the source of their power. If some person or organization tries to control or hinder that power, they will gather forces to eliminate that threat.

This is the cause of all these attacks, and honestly, they have gone farther than just bashing me with words. I am offering a way to teach people to heal themselves naturally, holistic remedies for depression and anxiety, different workout regimens to promote all around health, healthy diets, and a plethora of other real basic human things which all affect our psychology. I do this all out of the love for my fellow human beings. Pharmaceutical companies like Proxy and Keno are not the only ones attacking me, don't forget about Santomon and McMill's. My promotion of all around health disrupts their wicked circle of sickness.

PN: Can you tell me about the Drug and Disorder Manifold?

Dr. P: The Drug and Disorder Manifold is just a term for the granulation of individuals' personalities. The pharmaceutical companies that make all these drugs cannot possibly make their greedy system stop, so what will happen is: the more and more doctors they get on board their money train, the more and more disorders they will come up with until every single human being on this planet will have a unique disorder exclusive to themselves. And the treatment will be just as exclusive, an individualized cocktail of chemicals that ultimately take everything human out of a person. We'll have a society of impoverished zombies with a few very rich puppeteers.

PN: So let me sum up your method. You teach your patients some basic psychology via philosophical and religious texts, have them exercise and eat right, and in the case of chemical imbalances you recommend holistic remedies.

Dr. P: That's it in a nutshell. It is very simple, but the problem with most simple things, there is a very complicated path to get there. This is why I must choose my patients. Some are not willing to commit themselves to self-reflection and self-repair. I also will not deal with extreme cases such as *bone fide paranoid* schizophrenia. There is much that modern science can do that I cannot. I admit all my shortcomings and do not try to pretend to fix every psychological ailment. I just focus on the disorders that can be helped without prescribed medication.

PN: One last question. There is a rumor that you are working on a psychology book for kids based on the methods you've been developing. Is this true or just a rumor?

Dr. P: Word spreads fast. It's true. I hope to have it published soon. I've also been working on a curriculum of psychology for teachers in middle school and high school. There is already some progress that has been made over the years in this realm, but I wanted to make something more integrated with the entire world, with all religions and cultures.

PN: Thank you again for your time.

Dr. P: Thank you.

Chapter 23: Funhouse Mirrors

One night after work, I picked Ana up from Demos. She had a stack of books collected from the booklist she made for me. On top was a book titled *The Ancient Sport.* It was a book about the history of competitive wrestling and other martial arts. Several others were handpicked by her for my interests. I had barely acknowledged the book list she had already made for me. I realized then, sifting through this stack of books, that she knew me better than I knew myself. This was proof of Ana's perceptiveness.

There was a book on gourmet cooking that even had meat recipes. In this way, and this way only, she was willing to rest her convictions aside for a moment, just for my interests. Amazing woman.

Books about all the different things I wanted to learn about. A book about revolutions called *Always Revolution*, a compendium of Roman and Greek culture, *A Brief History of Socialism and Anarchism*, an enormous book on world mythology, and a few more.

I watched her show me each book, one by one, in that dimly lit warehouse portion of the co-op. She was smiling and looking me in the eye with each book explanation. I could only smile back. I had wanted to apologize incessantly, but I went with the moment, watching every facial movement on her beautiful and boney little face. She was perfect to me, with or without hair.

I carried the stack of books and Ana walked next to me with her arm on my lower back. She told me the story of when St. Catherine of Siena cut her hair. St. Catherine had felt enraptured with Jesus and God after cutting her hair in defiance of her parents, mainly her father, who wanted her to marry her sister's widower. She said that this was how she felt when she cut her hair, but her sense of divinity was with her own deity, her own Goddess, her namesake, Ana.

Ana the Starved One, the Loving One, the Infertile Cosmic Daughter, the One that bore all plights set by Man against the Earth and Mankind Itself.

"This Ana that I speak of, she is not like Jesus in one very particular way, she does not forgive mankind." Ana said.

"Do you forgive me?" I asked.

"Of course I do. I love you. So much."

***

It felt like forever since we last made love, but it had only been four days.

When we got home, she gave me some aromatic honey candy made by Devi. It was her gentle way of trying to mask any of the offensive odors that I had always floating about me. We got upstairs and she lit some candles.

She was intent on having me, she dragged me up the steps. She kissed and caressed me and removed our clothes. I barely had a chance to return my affection. I had forgotten everything in that moment.

She suddenly stopped, atop me. I was on my knees, inside her. Her tiny belly touching mine. She clutched her face with both hands. It happened too fast for her to react.

Puke flew out of the sides of her hands, I didn't flinch. It didn't bother me, I just felt instantly sorry for her. She was so embarrassed. She got up and stood for a moment, confused and crying. The shower was downstairs. She didn't know what to do.

I was sincerely sympathetic and caring. I grabbed the sheet of the bed and wrapped her in it and told her to go downstairs to the shower.

"I'll take care of it." I said.

I turned on the light and started cleaning what little puke there was. Barely any got on me, not that I cared anyway. I was really concerned for her. The situation made me realize that she had been eating, she had been trying to be healthy.

Out of habit, I inspected the vomit. How well she chewed her food, vegetable puree. Coincidentally, one of the books she had gotten for me was written by The Great Masticator himself, Horace Fletcher. I didn't know of him at that time, but he dedicated his life to studying eating habits and fecal matter for the good of the health of humankind.

I went down to the bathroom, indifferent to my nakedness. Ana was silently sobbing, trying to regain composure. I went into the shower with her and held her, she cried in my arms.

We were drying off and she kept apologizing.

"Don't apologize. It doesn't bother me at all." I said.

"It bothers me. I feel like a fool." She was drying me off. "And look at me. I'm a mess." She pointed at the long mirror on the door, at both of our reflections.

"You're beautiful." I caressed her head with my hand.

"Do you see this Jacob? Do you see how sick I look?"

"No."

"Then you're delusional. Can't you see how thin I am? I can see it. I could never see it before. I was delusional. I spent so many years of my life thinking I was a fat disgusting pig like all the rest of these people. But now I can see me for what I am, I'm a skeleton. How can a skeleton carry a baby into this world? Tell me that." She said. She put my hand on her belly, on that little bulb of life.

"I don't know. I just know that I love you."

"But love isn't going to fix this. I love you so much, and still I can't eat enough for this baby."

That was the first time I heard her use the term 'baby'.

"I used to think that my perceptions of myself were like being in a funhouse. I was always standing in front of that fat mirror. All I'd see was this fat ugly blob of flesh, this despicable excuse. But I can see reality now and I'm so afraid." She started to cry again then suddenly stopped. She abruptly looked mean.

"And what do you see?" She said and pointed at my belly, at my lump of fat under my bellybutton.

"I think I need to start running and working out more, but otherwise I haven't been worrying about it." I said.

"You're getting fat Jacob, and you don't even know it. You think bulimia is going to fix your problem? It's only making it worse. You have an eating problem, seriously. Didn't you think I'd notice?" She said.

I looked at us both in the mirror. I didn't get angry. She was right. And I was still feeling sympathetic enough to rationally listen to her.

My self-perception was certainly off, but then again whose isn't? When something is missing, our brains fill it in. When something is excessive, our brains can magically take it away. We do it all the time. But with our bodies and our entire beings, it's a two-way street.

On the phone, our ears pick up fragments of what is actually said and our brain fills in the rest. Our eyes do it with optical illusions. But with our body image, we can add and subtract whatever we want to suit our own insecurities and hubris. Males can magically make their penises bigger or smaller and likewise so can females change their breast or buttocks size and even change the look of their vulva. We change who we are.

When I was going through puberty, I was always on the search for the new body change. When I didn't have pubic hair, I searched for each new hair. In the armpits, the same. I'd search for new muscle definition, practically every day. I spent an incredible amount of time in the mirror, looking for that new change, that new thing that made me more of a man, the split in the pectoral muscles, the crease in the biceps and triceps, the six-pack abs.

I flexed and held my breath till I almost passed out, just looking for veins to pop out of my shoulders and my forearms.

This was my adolescence, searching for my body to become a man. When each new change arrived, I sought out the next. And at last I found that ever-present pinch on my tummy, that camel's hump that did not go away. Even at 5% body fat that damned lump was still there.

In this mirror with Ana, me and my fatty lump and her with her life-begetting bulb stood there hand in hand. We were by no means on the same level, she was so far beyond me. My ignorance at that time kept me from knowing the truth of the matter, and how serious her situation really was.

'We'll be okay,' was all that my ignorant and cocky self could muster. It was all that my broken record of make-believe brain could think to say to this divine woman.

She slept with her head on my chest, my arm around her. We woke up the same way.

***

I went for a jog in the morning, instantly out of breath. The early sun was harsh and I broke a sweat on my walk to the river. My body felt weak and pathetic. After jogging, I did some push-ups and sit-ups, a once easy task now difficult.

My mind kept repeating the things Ana had said. I was trying to digest everything. I was motivated by the thought of Ana's strength. She was fighting a war with herself, mentally and physically. And meanwhile, I was still wrapped up in my petty vanity, even with her candid pleas. I was only pretending to understand the weight of the situation.

When I got back, Ana was leaving. "I'll be right back." She said and kissed me as she left. She was wearing make-up as usual, but something was different. The stuff around her eyes wasn't smooth and fine but thick and blotchy. She had briefly mentioned something about making her own make-up, so she had. I really thought it looked rough and pharaoh-like. I always told her she didn't need it, and she really didn't, shaved-head or not. She was that beautiful to me, every moment. The puking and the crying and the shower created situations that were beyond her control. She proved she was eating in the most humiliating way, yet she still looked sickly. She hadn't been able to hide what she really looked like. Under the mask she had deep dark rings around her eyes, permanent makeup. Her skin was blotchy and blemished, she really didn't look healthy, but my heart was my vision then, and she looked perfectly fine to me.

I was reading *The Last Waif: Or, Social Quarantine* by Horace Fletcher. Horace Fletcher was called the 'The Great Masticator'. He devoted his time studying human excreta and eating habits to compile theories about the diet of a human. He would have loathed both Ana and I.

The Last Waif was the topmost book on Ana's stack of books, our stacks lay next to each other, and I couldn't help myself but to snoop. I had thought a *waif* was something they called skinny models that were gaining popularity and criticism in my teens, not the case. I looked it up in the huge dictionary Ana had brought from the co-op. Among the definitions were phrases like 'without home or friends' and 'an outcast from society' and 'unowned and neglected child'.

Ana came home while I was paging through *The Last Waif*, the section was about government's responsibility to make fine *status quo* orphans.

"Believe it or not, I used to be a fan of Fletcherism." Ana said. She set down a wooden thing resembling a briefcase and a bag of fluff. "I chew my food thirty-three times, once more than Fletcher's recommendation. And I don't eat when I'm angry or upset. Otherwise, Fletcher was just like all the other rich orthorexics, stingy and vain. Dr. Kellogg was far worse though, can you imagine that the inventor of cornflakes was a racist crusader against sex? Something was terribly wrong with that guy, vegetarian or not."

'Chew your food until it swallows itself', Mr. Fletcher would have told you if he was your counselor at the FTC. He would have also told you that his shit doesn't stink (using the word *excreta* instead of *shit*), because he believed that a perfectly healthy body should release odorless excreta.

Ana and her best friend Mary joked about 'eating like a Horace' when they were barely thirteen. They were young and proud to be anorexic together, or if not pride, they found comfort with their disease through their friendship. They had met in the FTC. For many times after that meeting, Ana was locked up when Mary was out, and vice versa. Their times together were short-lived but wonderful.

Mary killed herself a year before I met Ana, she sliced her wrists with a paper thin blade of a shaving razor, along the tracks so to speak. This gave Ana a new meaning to Fletcher's piece of clever advice. Before Mary died, Ana hadn't seen her for six months.

The FTC had chewed Mary up until she swallowed herself. This was one of the turning points in Ana's personal revolution starting with the FTC and ending with mankind itself.

Mary killed herself the same day Ana had gotten released, yet again, from FTC. Ana's new foster mother forbade her to leave. Ana left anyway, barged out the door. Hours too late, she found out the news.

'If I believed in violence, I would certainly blow up the FTC and the building that's home to the Bureau of Orphan Neglect. Without all the people in it of course.' Ana said this a few times, always in reference to Mary's death. She didn't believe in violence, but she did say that she would like to kill Mary's foster father. Mary was sexually abused for years, and unlike Ana, she was frail on the inside as well as the outside. No one ever believed her. She was that crazy orphan child who talked to herself. I saw Ana at her angriest about the subject of Mary.

Both Mary and Ana made desperate attempts to get Mary out of the foster home she was in but nothing ever happened. All five personnel that made up the mighty Bureau of Orphan Neglect (they called themselves 'bone') was under the spell of the patriarch of the household, a wealthy politician. Coincidentally, the FTC was run by a corporate executive that used to be friends with Mary's foster father when they were at the same prestigious university together.

Ana sat next to me as I was finishing the page I was reading. "I only grabbed this book because of Mary. I'm beyond anything Fletcher had to say. I never read one of his books anyway. Mary and I only read his stuff out of a dieting book we liked, called *The Power of Thin*."

"So what's in the brief case?" I asked.

"It's a *charkha*." She said. "It's a spinning wheel like the one that Gandhi used to spin cotton for his cloth. This particular one is a book charkha. It was a vital tool in India's revolution. A bigger version is like the one that's on India's flag."

Ana opened the charkha up, just like a suitcase. It looked antique and fragile. She grabbed the bag of cotton and started setting up. I watched, intrigued.

"Devi gave this to me. She's been teaching me about fiber arts since I met her, and quite a bit about India and Gandhi. She's also going to get me a home loom. Then I can start making you some new clothes."

"I've got clothes at my mom's house. I just have to go pick them up." I said.

"What good are those clothes to your revolution? They were made by sweatshop slaves, from the farm to the factory. We need to be wearing homespun cloth, like Mahatma. We need to change the things in ourselves if we want to change the world." She was smiling and at peace. She was turning a wheel with one hand and holding a line of thread from a ball of cotton.

I grabbed the book *The Ancient Sport* from the top of my stack and went back to reading, watching her out of the corner of my eye.

Ana was spinning on the charkha while singing one of her many songs. Her siren voice distracted me even further from reading.

If I wasn't looking at her, I was looking at the pictures of ancient examples of wrestling and boxing. The Greeks called it *pankration,* or 'all strengths'. Most ancient civilizations have some sort of competition than is related to wrestling, some include punching. Most of these competitions are done in the sand. The sand disperses the impact of the bodies when they land.

She stopped singing to tell me about that she didn't consider herself anorexic anymore. "Anorexia is a condition concerning self-perception and self-imposed starvation. Our own perverse and distorted thinking is at the root of our eating disorders. I feel that I'm beyond that. If I have an eating disorder anymore, I would name it Ana-ism. If I had a mental disorder, it would be the Gandhi Complex. But I wouldn't call it a disorder. It's an order, to stop the injustice in the world."

Ana-ism is my religion. It will have a few premises. One must be a fructarian or frugivore, which essentially means that one must never harm anything living for food. One must never eat of animal flesh even if the animal has fallen of natural causes. This carnivorous action itself is violent.

One must never use currency, ever. One must not hoard any goods or knowledge, one must not be a *dragon*. There are a few more I'm working on, but that's it in a nutshell." She said, still spinning. She giggled. "The difference between Gandhi and I is that he loved and defended his people, but I on the other hand can't shake this disgust I have for my people and their pitiful culture and ignorance, regardless of how peaceful I'm trying to be in action."

I wanted to ask her about the pregnancy but couldn't force the words out of my mouth. She couldn't possibly plan on having an abortion, but we hadn't discussed anything about actually having a child, what we would do? I couldn't ask her. We had such a rough night that I didn't want to spoil the time with my concerns. I wanted to ask her 'where would our child fit in this revolution of yours?', but I knew what she would say. 'Right between us.'

'And as for sex,' she said, 'sex should be kind and gentle, as non-violent as possible."

***

I woke from a dream that night.

I dreamt of wrestling my father on top of a mountain in a lightning storm. He was drunk and easily maneuvered, and yet he was too strong for me to throw him down the mountain. Cy was suddenly there helping me. Finally, our father slipped and we switched to helping him, but he slipped from my hand and plummeted down the mountainside into the abyss. The abyss was a dark ocean with reflections of my mother's crystalline face everywhere on the sparkling black waves. My brother disappeared and I sat there on the mountain as it grew quickly away from the shore of the ocean.

I woke up sweaty and thirsty. I was chugging down water out of a gallon from the fridge when Cy walked in. I could tell he was hammered, but he kept his composure as usual. The man had the mental fortitude of a Titan.

When we were kids, he got hit in the head with a rock and got a second degree concussion. He was hit hard enough to knock an adult out, but he only wobbled a bit, regained his composure, and chased the kid down for revenge.

"What are you doing tomorrow morning?" Cy asked.

"I have to work at three." I said.

“We’re going to install that toilet first. Dude’s dropping it off at nine. Then I’ll need your help with a few other things.” He said. “I offered David a place to stay. I figured you wouldn’t mind. He’ll be here in the morning.”

“I don’t mind at all. I was going to ask you anyway. You should see that place. It’s a landfill.” I said.

“I will. I’m going to pick him up tomorrow.”

***

I woke up around nine. I could hear Cy and his friend talking out in the backyard. I woke Ana up and headed downstairs to help.

The sun was a halo on a distant rooftop and the air smelled of cut-grass, not yet the midday garbage smell. Lawnmowers puttered away, an angry mother was yelling at kids or dogs or her husband, a couple was drunk and fighting, a continuation from the night before.

My brother and his friend were talking and staring down at the toilet bowl and tank like they were parts of a felled beast. They were both already drinking beer and talking loud. He introduced me to his friend then they went back to talking about the ’69 Mercury Cougar. They did this for hours, it was Saturday. My father did the same thing, drink beer all day and fix or make things.

David was sitting cross-legged and feeding the neighbor’s cats pieces of his sandwich through the fence.

“How many cats does this lady have?” David asked.

“I’ve counted 29, but I’m not sure. There are a few that look the same so it’s hard to know exactly.” I said.

“Have you met the lady?”

"A few times. Her name is Judith and she doesn't hear very well. I had to say my name more than ten times only to have her respond with a different name each time. I gave up and now she calls me Caleb." I said.

He laughed. "Caleb means dog in Hebrew which is funny because the Bible always refers to dogs negatively, even funnier coming from a cat lady."

"Did you go back to the landfill?" I asked.

"Yeah, I had to grab the rest of my stuff. Good timing too, because the place was being condemned by the city. Like I said before, someone should just burn the thing down and start all over."

"I'm glad you're out of there. Fresh start?" I said.

"Yes, fresh start." David said. "Do you need help with the toilet?"

"I'll let you know. *Fiat Lux?*"

"You like that?" David said.

"What does it mean?"

"Let there be light."

Cy told me that I could remove the old one and help him install the new one. I grabbed the tools off the new toilet.

"I shut the water off already, so everything should be good to go. Grab a bucket and some towels on your way up and come get me if you got any problems." He said and tossed me and David a beer. I had a feeling Ana wasn't going to like me drinking beer around her, but there was a part of me that rebelled.

"You're drinking beer this early?" Ana said. She was whizzing away on the charkha.

"Yeah, so." I said. Jacob the Rebel.

"You know the smell bothers me for one, and for two, I thought we were going to spend time together later." She said. Ana the Mother.

"It's just a beer."

"You're an alcoholic Jacob. I don't care if you drink once a year, you don't know when to stop. You're better off not drinking at all." She said.

"How do you know? You don't know everything. You think you do, but you don't." I said. Jacob, his father's son.

"I know what's best for you at nine thirty in the morning. An apple and a glass of water." She said.

"You go eat an apple! You're the one who needs it." I said.

I cracked the beer and chugged half of it. I was kneeling next to the toilet and tightening the water valves.

Ana started quietly crying and packing up her charkha.

"You don't want to help me get better do you?" She stood over me fighting her cry.

"You don't want to get better. If you really wanted to, you would. And how can I help you?" I stopped to take a chug of beer. I didn't look at her. I knew I was wrong and that ignorant and stubborn part of myself took over. I stood up, looking at the toilet.

"You want me to listen, I listen. When you want me to do something for you, I do it. When you tell me there is something wrong with the world, I try to understand and in ways I'm trying to be who you want me to be. But I won't just let you tell me how I'm going to live or what I'm going to think. You're not my mom!"

Only then did I look at her and my face felt monstrous. "And even my mom can't tell me what to do anymore."

"I'm sorry if I come off the way I do. I thought you'd be a bit more considerate. I thought we cared about many of the same causes. I guess you're just as selfish and apathetic as the rest of these so called rebels." She said.

I was concentrating on the toilet and what I had to do to disconnect it. I was diverting my anger.

"So you're just going to ignore me?"

"I have nothing to say to you." I said.

"You never do. You never tell me what's bothering you. You assume so much about me, and that you don't have to say, I can sense it. Well, we are going to have to talk. We're always going to have to talk, if we're ever going to be happy together." She said and left.

I drank the rest of the beer and took the toilet apart. We decided on leaving the high tank and pull chain for decoration.

I questioned myself why the toilet was so important for me to get replaced. It was in the wide open, and I never shit or pissed in front of Ana, let alone puke. She insisted that we stay up there in that smoldering sauna. She didn't mind the heat, it reminded her of India or Ethiopia. It reminded me of passing out in the steam-room trying to lose weight. I did mind but as with most things, I just kept my mouth shut and sucked it up.

She always drank water up there. She survived up there, on air and water, the Ethiopian diet. If and when she ate, I never knew.

Ana had a power inside herself that I never had. She would have refused the Santomon genetically modified corn they sent in to help with the Ethiopian famine because of her beliefs and rightly so. This was the same cornmeal that was indigestible to all those starving people. They made a fatal mistake in not mentioning to starving people that cornmeal needs to be processed with lime or some other type of acid so that humans can digest it. Many bellies swelled to death from charity corn. If you are what you eat, those poor kids were exploding like popcorn, their feeble bodies trying to ruminate with single out-of-practice stomachs. Even if they were fed proper food, they could die from Refeeding Syndrome, when the starving body dies from digestion.

Santomon, Proxy and Keno, McMill's, and the rest, they all pretend to care. They send their poisoned food and give children mind-altering medication and feed them nutrition-less, glamorized food. But in this life, it is not in the spirit of genuine caring. It's for profit. At your most vulnerable time, when you're depressed and someone has died or your wife left you, all you need is a hug. But sometimes a hug can be a choke, a slow and fatal choke.

Ana was strengthening her convictions daily. Her diet was already fructarian, as in Jainism, and that of the utopian people she told me about in Samuel Butler's book *Erehwon,* and Gandhi. 'One must only eat the fruit or seed of a plant that has shed it.', was one of her new commandments of Ana-ism. Corn had to be harvested, and like other grains, Ana felt that this should be forbidden.

Who was I to question her convictions when I had none of my own? Me, my father's son, an angry destroyer incapable of crying or communicating emotions.

I removed the toilet bowl and carried it downstairs. My chin rested on the lid and I walked down the stairs. Good bye old, hello new. My mind was calling out for drunkenness, for void.

I got downstairs and set the toilet down next to the new one. Everybody was watching me. They saw Ana leave in a fury. My brother threw me a beer and we all stood around the toilets. Out of respect, no one asked what happened or what's wrong, this was the standard for the men's club. I was glad for this.

We drank the day away into deep night. Beer and booze and talking. Then we wrestled in the pankration pit. The din of our shouts and grunts matched the backdrop of gunshots and quarrels.

David had his notebook, and while he could, he wrote what I can't remember.

***

Jacob wrestled himself and God.

In sands of the timeless arena, we grappled with the laws of our ancestors under the raven sky of glimmering eyes made from both stars and spectators.

We wrestled one another out of defiance of the nations that no longer fight weaponless,we wrestled to cease our descendents' vile history.

Life-mongering cowards, all those that seek death for enemies whom they are supposed to love.

The faceless crowd, a crescendo of din. The lights, artificial and salient.

Did we ever need hatred? Out of our differences, to grow, to flourish?

As David, the conqueror of those who defied the tribe of He-who-wrestles-with-God, let me be forgiven that I did not try to find a peaceful way sooner.

Shall I ever again smite my enemy and sever his head for the sake of my people?

Nay, never.

All of you, my people, none excluded, can we say "Never Again?"

For we are of a different time when we need not kill each other over dominion of the earth. We are one tribe.

Let us contest equally Goliath and stay our weapons, as equals, as brothers, while our brother wrestles with himself.

The Path of God is the Path of the Self, under and over and through the Self, the entirety from within and without.

***

I was barely able to function at work the next day. Cy's 'care package' barely got me out the door. When I got to the Epicurean, the dishes were piled up in my area and Chef Jeff was trying to catch them up. I was late an hour.

"Chef John is pissed at you, so I recommend that you don't go back by his office." Chef Jeff said.

I worked my hardest considering how I felt. Dish after dish, leftovers of appetizers and entrees and desserts all down the disposal. Only when I got caught up did I start shoveling some of the choice leftovers in my maw.

The lunch rush had slowed so I took my time with each plate that arrived. I was busy gnawing on a seared lamb chop when the maître'd came up to my busing window.

"What are you doing?" The maître'd said. He never came to the busing window. In fact I had only talked to him a few times. He was apparently angry at what I was doing.

I shrugged.

"A very important customer saw you and was threatening to call the State Health Department. I had to give him a month's worth of complimentary meals. Do you know how much that is going to cost the restaurant? I've yet to tell Chef John, but I can almost guarantee that you'll be terminated for this."

I kept eating. I didn't care, and I didn't like his attitude.

"You're disgusting."

Chef John didn't approach me. He had Jacques come tell me to go home for the day and that I wasn't fired, yet.

"And rich people act surprised when revolutions happen. 'Let them eat cake.' Marie Antoinette said. 'Off with your filthy rich head,' is what the poor people said. Screw that guy. What does he care about what we do with their garbage anyway?" Jacques said.

Chapter 24: Cat at the Scale of Heart

David and I were wrestling in the sand pit under the evening sun. The sand coated our sweaty skin like we were powdered doughnuts. I was learning different take-downs that I had never heard of from the book *The Ancient Sport* keeping in mind some of the things Cy had told me.

Cy was at the Cornerstone, resting.

Ana was at Devi's house. She was having fierce abdominal pains and they were both trying to figure out the best herb to use. She was gone longer than usual.

"Have you ever wrestled your brother?" David asked.

"Yeah, since he's been training me. And it's the same as when we were kids. There's no competition. I wouldn't even call it wrestling." I said.

"There wasn't one thing I could do, he just grabbed me up and I was done. I would have to use a sling and he'd probably laugh after he got hit in the head." David said.

"He outweighs you by a hundred pounds, and he's a great wrestler. Don't sweat it."

"Damned Goliath. It would be the reverse of the story, because I'm technically a dirty Philistine, I still have my foreskin."

"Well, it's never too late, is it? I'm sure there is someone around here who can do a backdoor circumcision." I said.

"Why were you guys circumcised anyway? Weren't you raised Catholic?" David asked.

"I never thought to ask. I just figured it was normal."

“Normal for Americans and Jews and Muslims. Most of the world is uncircumcised. But there is a tribe in Papua New Guinea that circumcises twice.” David said.

“What’s the second one suppose to be?” I asked.

“You don’t want to know.”

Ana had arrived with a dead cat in her arms. It was a seal point Himalayan. Ana was crying and looking me in the eyes. “Sofia’s dead.” She said. “She was hit by a car.”

I rushed over to her. I put my hand on her shoulder and looked down at the cat. I didn’t know that any of them had names, let alone which one was named what. Ana had talked with Judy the Catlady frequently, mostly about her cats. This wasn’t even a rare occurrence. A stray pitbull nabbed one up every now and then. This particular occurrence was witnessed by Ana. She held Sofia during her last breath.

“I can’t stand these cars. These evil things. They are nothing but destruction. Omnicidal weapons that function off of a commodity that brings the most death to all.” She said.

She was right. In America, they are more dangerous than guns. And when there is a modern war, it’s about oil or rubber. Don’t get Ana started on oil.

“Do you want me to bury her?” I asked.

“No.” Ana said.

“Do you want me to build a pyre down by the river?” I said.

“No, I was thinking of mummification. Can you do that for me given that you’re a hunter?”

“I don’t know where to start. I only know what I’ve seen in the museum.” I said.

"One of the books I got you has how the Egyptians did it. Herodotus wrote about it. I would do it myself but I don't think I could stomach it. Holding this dear soul is hard enough right now." Ana said. "I want her heart to be weighed against the Feather of Truth, because I know it's true unlike us humans."

David came over and stood by us. "Mummification is perfect. Thousands of years from now, future peoples can dig up our civilization and find this anomaly. The archeologists will say to themselves, 'Look here, someone cared about an animal more than objects."

"If I'm going to do this, I have to do it now. She'll rot quickly in this heat."

I grabbed my Survival Rucksack, a box of canning salt, *The Histories* by Herodotus, and the glass knife then we all went to the river. I told Ana to stay home, but she insisted. She wanted to see, to experience the reality of the deceased. She didn't want to hide from death. She wanted to see the internals of a victim of the unnatural.

***

We went to the spot where David and I had 'dressed' and skinned Felicitas the fox. I strung her up and stood there thinking. I was afraid to do it. A strange feeling overcame me. I had only dealt with hunted animals, never pets. I had pets that died when I was a kid, but we buried them. I kept thinking about how it would be to deal with a friend or family member's body. My dad talked about 'dealing with your dead', but he never took active steps in acquiring information on how to do it. If he did, he didn't tell me or Cy about it.

I had David read aloud the section in *The Histories* by Herodotus that dealt with Egyptian mummification.

"It says here that we should cover the body with *natrum*, or sodium carbonate for seventy days." David said.

"We can use baking soda for now. I'll call my dad. He used to be a taxidermist." I said.

I got over myself and my feelings. I pretended that Ana wasn't behind me watching. The moment I slit the skin, my brain shut down into the unemotional and mindless concentration. I imagined that morticians think this way. This was a state of mind I had learned throughout the years of killing and eating animals, the detachment of compassion for another living being. The survivor omnivore, the destroyer of all things, the omnicidal maniac, the bringer of the terrestrial omniclusion, the Human.

"What should I do with the organs?" I said.

"Leave it for scavengers." Ana said. Her voice was weak.

Ana walked home. David and I stayed to clean up the mess.

"Keep the intestines." I said.

"What?" David said.

"I can use them for lyre strings."

***

I called the general store that my dad called from every Sunday. The owner went and fetched him from the bar and had him call back.

I picked up the ringing phone.

"Hello Dad."

"Hello Jacob. It's been awhile. I was going to come back to town and get you out of that nuthouse, but I heard you were already out by the time I could leave. "

"I know, Cy told me."

"What was your mom thinking? She should have put herself in there, she's the one who's crazy. And what's this I hear about you puking to be skinny. Isn't that a girl thing?"

"It was for wrestling, to make weight in wrestling. I didn't call to talk about that. I just have a quick question for you." I said.

"Shoot."

"I'm trying to mummify a cat. What should I use to preserve it?"

"I'm not going to ask why, but it sounds interesting. Borax is what you want. You can buy Ten Oxen Borax at the local store. That should deplete the body of anything that will putrefy."

"One other question. Where can I find pine or cedar resin?" I said.

"Use shellac. You can buy it at the hardware store."

Don't get Ana started on shellac, the preserve made from thousands of crushed beetles.

"I need resin." I said.

"I'm not sure where you can buy it but you can harvest that yourself. Just strip enough bark on a pine or cedar tree to make a channel then put a tin ramp at the bottom. Nail a bucket to catch the sap. Then you have to boil it for a long time to separate the liquid. You'd be better off doing this outside." He said.

"Thanks. That's all I need."

"Okay. I'll call you when I come back into town or you can call me here at the general store. And if you want to get away from that dirty old city and live the real life, you're always welcome. We've got a nice little village started. We even installed bunkers for when the nukes drop. All we need now are some women, that's all. They all think we're crazy, they'll soon see."

"Well, I have to go dad before that body putrefies."

“Okay son. I love you. Goodbye.”

“Live in this world Dad.” I said.

“Yeah, not the next.” He said.

“Go with God.” I said, my brother’s brother.

I hung up.

My brother came home meanwhile and handed me a beer. I cracked it. Ana walked away and went upstairs with her head down.

“Ana, we’ll need to have linen in seventy days.” I said.

“That won’t be a problem.” She said down the stairs.

Cy went to the store to get the borax.

I had packed Sophia in a wooden wine box full of baking soda down by the river. I removed the clumping pink and white powder into the garbage. Her fur was matted, she was stiff.

David stood and watched me. We were silent. I drank another beer.

I removed the brains by drilling a hole at the top of the skull and suctioned them out with a basting syringe. Every so often an emotion plowed through me, and I drank some more.

The Egyptians removed the brain through the nose. They also believed that the heart was the organ for thinking, and for good reason.

After Cy got back with the borax, I stuffed her with it. I had to hand stitch her abdomen closed and her eyelids shut. I put her in a pine winebox I saved from work. She stayed that way for seventy days in the fetal position just like she came to this world, in her mother’s womb.

***

Chef John cut my hours in half. He wanted to let things smooth over with the angry rich customer who caught me eating his leftovers.

I had more time to spend with Ana, and if I wasn't with her, I was wrestling or working on the house with Cy and David.

For days after the death of Sofia, Ana and I had little conversation. She sang her somber songs, but the vitality of her voiced diminished with each day. She was suffering far more than I knew, and I was being a stubborn ass with what I felt, shoving the feelings aside. I showed some affection for how could I not? Ana was my heart.

I spent time making a lyre out of wood I found by the river and the intestines of Sophia for strings. No easy task when using handmade stone tools. I tried modeling it after the ones on the Greek wine jugs displayed in *Dr. Mantha's Compendium of Myth and Legend.* It ended up being a piss-poor replica, and the sound was strange. I didn't know how it should sound, I had never heard one played.

When I finished the lyre, I attempted to play along with Ana's music, she didn't mind though I couldn't match her notes.

Ana had lost the ambition to go for walks or even to sit down by the river. She was lethargic and weak. I worried and said nothing.

Ana and I worked together in our attic room. She weaved on her loom and I played my lyre.

Every morning she made trips to visit Devi for textile items and holistic remedies for the pains she was having.

I carded cat fur from the Persian cats next door. Carding is brushing fiber with two oversized brushes. Only an hour or two of this work was all I could handle at a time. It wasn't meditation to me like it was for Ana. The rest of the time I played my pale version of a lyre and read bits and pieces of the books she brought me.

Near the last days, Ana didn't sing anymore, yet she weaved and I still played.

Ana processed flax for weeks and a small amount of fine fiber came from all of her efforts. From plant to cloth, she wove enough linen to make me a gift.

She made me a *langot*, Indian underwear used in India's ancient wrestling sport, *Pehlwani.* It was dyed reddish brown with henna. At first I was uncomfortable about wrestling in it, there was an emphasis on my male package like a jockstrap. But then I thought of the Greeks and Romans and how they wrestled naked. Or even in modern times, the singlets we had to wear that showed the audience the spectacle of your genitalia, I got over it. It was perfect for wrestling in, no restrictions.

Ana had to teach me to tie the *langot* which required me being naked. Before she could finish tying it, we made love for the last time. It was sweet and slow, effortless love, barely moving.

When she finished using flax fiber, she had a brilliant idea, spinning Persian cat fur for weaving. What better cloth to mummify a cat with but the fur of Sophia's extended family?

We went over and asked Judith if we could comb her cats for their fur. She was more than happy to let us, and even better, she had been saving all the fur for a few years. She was constantly grooming her Persian cats due to the heat and their frequent dreadlocks that developed. This fur source was an endless supply considering half of her thirty odd cats were Persian or similar long hair breeds. She brought out bags and bags of the stuff. She knew there was a reason she was saving it. Judith was a packrat, cat-ladies are often packrats. What she didn't want though, was the mummified version of Sophia. *That*, she wanted Ana to keep.

We had developed a miniature textile workshop up there in our attic. David came and helped with carding or spinning. David did most of the talking when he was around. He apologized for talking so much, we assured him it was okay. 'I reserve silence for when I'm by myself which has been often in the last few months.' He had told us.

Ana had been constantly spinning and weaving and was volunteering less and less at Demos. She barely even read books anymore. Her first fabric was made from the first cotton fibers she had spun on her charkha. This piece, along with two more she wove were strips of fabric which became her only clothing.

"The nuns and monks in Jainism can only wear white non-stitched clothing, and some wear no clothing at all. They call it 'Clothing of the Sky'. I wouldn't mind being naked all the time, but I don't think you would like that very much. And other people would just think I was a skeleton who swallowed a grapefruit, a *Hunger Artist*. Then they would commit me for sure. Who wants to arrest a skeleton for indecent exposure." Ana said.

She was moving the shuttle between two taut planes of fibers then shifting and clicking the loom.

"I wouldn't mind inside the house. I'd probably get jealous if everyone got to see you naked." I said.

"Jealous of what? You don't own me. I'm not your private piece of meat." She said. She sounded passive despite the words.

"I don't think I own you. I'm just being honest. I think I would have a problem with it. That's my own insecurity I'd have to deal with." I said.

"Jealousy comes from your violence. And your whole life is violence, Jacob. You need to think about that, seriously. I know you are a man and I forgive you for the violent things you enjoy in this life. But I don't want our child to inherit all of your violence. I'm not talking about everything either. I engage in violence just by being with you and having sex with you. Even talking is a violent act when you break it all down. We need to start working on how we are going to be as parents." Ana said.

"I have thought about it. I have to find a better job or hope for a raise. They might fire me anyway." I said.

"You don't need to work for those capitalists. It doesn't have to be that way. You're still suffering from the programming of consumerism. Believe it or not, we can sustain ourselves on very little. The neighborhood marketplace can sustain us for most things, and the rest we can do on our own. We don't have to participate in the violence of capitalism." Ana said.

"How are we going to pay for rent. We can't just leech off of my brother forever, and I can't barter homespun cat-fur cloth for the rest of our days. I don't like this society either, but it doesn't mean we can just take ourselves out of it completely." I said.

"Your brother said that you didn't have to pay him if you couldn't as long as you help him with the house. And I can help with certain things. If we convert you pankration pit into another garden then we could have a decent portion of food, and the rest we can get from Devi. She could feed half of this neighborhood with her greenhouses and gardens."

"That's sounds so pleasant and responsible, but this is all new to me. I still like things in this world, and I haven't made the change to be free of wanting to do or have certain things. I'm not at your level." I said.

"You know that quote from Gandhi, 'Be the change that you want to see in the world.' What change do you want in the world Jacob? I know you want everyone to be able to survive without technology, and I love you for that. But the world hasn't ended yet. When you think it's almost finished, we'll still keep destroying everything. What are you trying to change for this world, what are you wanting to be?"

"I don't know Ana. I really don't. I'm sorry I'm an idiot. I have been learning from you and trying to be how you are, but I have a whole life before you that I can't just throw away so easily. For years, wrestling has been my life. I know you think it's shallow and violent. But that's who I am. What I have been. I am this stupid male who destroys this world, but I'm trying to change that. Everyday, I try. But sometimes I fail." I said.

"I never called you an idiot Jacob. You've made so many changes for me and I thank you for that, but I can't participate in the violence in this world. And I don't want our child to participate in it either. I can't change your mind though. That's completely up to you." Ana said.

Chapter 25: Fetus/Flush

Of course, I was genuflecting at the toilet, praying to the proverbial porcelain God, when I got that last phone call from Ana. I was wiping my face and pinching the lump of fat folding over my pants. Probably at 15% body fat. A whole 10 percent more than when I went to the FTC. Wrestling didn't cross my mind. I could only brood over how Ana was right. Ana was always right. She had told me that bulimia is fine if you're not hyperphagic like I was. Too many calories. Ana had to teach me what a calorie was and that vodka has lots of them.

Of all the partial meals and desserts I consumed for that vomit session, the ones I remember consisted of 4 ounces of beef tartar, the very end of veal Wellington, two pork tenderloin medallions, and a ramekin of crème brule with a spoonful missing. I wasn't concerned with the world at that time. I wasn't concerned about the caged and cute calves. I didn't care about the beakless chickens pumped with steroids. I didn't care about the rich and wannabe rich that followed their own etiquette of wastefulness. I was wrapped-up Selfishness and Anger, seasoned by my addictions, my diseases. Jake Wellington smothered in self-loathing cream sauce.

Ana and I had our last argument that horrible day and then shortly thereafter, our last conversation. I had bottled up everything from the prior couple weeks and it all came out in one explosive outburst.

I had set a mental deadline for Ana to abort our fetus. It was my own calculation based on when she conceived. Three months, give or take a week. Jacob the Pathetic Insecure Ignorant Boy With No Ears. If only I had listened to her, truly and sincerely listened, I would have known that she had every intention of bringing our baby into this world.

Her words echo eternal in my head. 'I'm not getting rid of *it.*'

I had spent the night drunk outside in the sandpit, puke for a blanket. My head was in a headlock of aching, my mouth a desert with real sand and all. I had a frightful dream of fighting my father with his slotted wood paddle named 'Punishment' and his asskicking boots called 'Shitkickers'. I was huddled in a corner, crying.

I went inside to shower and get ready for work. Ana was standing there, flouncing. I was still drunk and didn't care.

“So it’s now or never.” I said. I pointed at her little bulb of a belly.

In a relationship, it is said that communication is key. I had no key and no idea of what was actually going on that day. Me, my father’s son, drunk and caring only of myself and worrying about the End of Days.

She was going to respond. I didn’t let her. I was the *man* of the hour. That spiteful, despicable *man* of the hour.

“You know we have a vacuum. It’d save us the money.” I said. My father’s son, a rotten apple not far from the rotten tree of apathy.

She was crying immediately. I was immune to the crying. I was raised with a mother crying, constantly crying. Girlfriends crying, and for a few months, Ana crying. On the outside, I was this immovable beast, but in truth I was nothing but a little child who was small and weak and scared of the world.

As usual, she quickly gained composure. Ana had been hurt so much in her life that she knew how to deal with it. And her values were so strong, she could not be defeated. Ana the Cosmic Daughter of Will.

I said a bunch of other dumb shit before she said her part.

“Don’t you think I would have aborted already? You haven’t listened to me since we fought about it. I’m trying to bring our baby to term Jacob. I’ve been eating in the all the ways I can. You don’t see me eat, but I have been. ”

She was still in tears. Her face was distorted like the first time I saw her. I remember that face so vividly beautiful, yet I know that I was flushed with my own selfish anger. I was the inconsiderate God of Anger and Anguish and Apathy.

“All you’ve done is ridicule me. All my beliefs. And me. You’re still hung up on that one moment when I considered having an abortion.

You haven't noticed that I do care about having our baby. You haven't tried to look. I have been trying to change what I do to myself for the sake of my cause, but I still endeavor to have this baby and me be healthy. Sometimes I wish I could eat more like you, but I can't. I can't binge on everything I see."

I was listening to her but not comprehending. I was completely full of myself. Completely full of shit.

"I know I'm hard to deal with. But I can't help the way I feel about this world. And I know you feel the same way, it's why I love you."

What I was doing was 'hearing' her, I wasn't listening.

"If I'm going to be healthy and carry our baby, I need your support. I need your help. I know I've turned down your food, but I'm trying to construct the best way to live in this decrepit society. In my head I feel I'm getting better though my body is still suffering."

What I was thinking at the time is more horrible than the words. But I said. "So who is the martyr in this whole hunger strike? The fetus or you?"

She was still trying to talk to me when I was showering and getting ready for work. I was being the ignorant and insensitive and insecure fool that I had been since I had met her. No one could forgive me for those moments, not for a thousand years of my apologies.

She didn't attack me as she did before. I was completely in the wrong and she was still reaching out for me. This was the girl that had the strongest will of anyone I have ever met, and she let it all go for a moment, just to be denied.

I didn't look at her when I left for work. I walked to work in my uncompromising tunnel of anger. So standing over the Sinkerator, between the Wash-o-matic and the busing window, I ate everything just to spite her. Jacob the Sinkerator. The veal, the chicken, the aspic engelled pork loin, everything in spite of her values and my newly adopted ones. Jacob the Devourer.

Ana called when I was in the bathroom sticking my emetic feather down my throat.

Only thinking of myself and the blood in my vomit, I told Chef Jeff that I'd call Ana back when I was done. Regretfully, I was only thinking of my own unhealthiness and that the blood in the vomit could only come from my stomach and not the veal Wellington or beef tartar. That little calf and its mother or father were already drained of their blood. I finished up and brushed my teeth then went to the phone.

"What do you want?"

"I'm miscarrying. Can you come home?" Ana was sincere, as always. I was a dick, the violent phallic weapon against Mother Nature. I was a puked-up hunk of half-chewed food, a piece of shit.

"When my shift ends. What do you need me for?" This was me.

"I just need you to be here."

"If it's that bad, call 911."

"Sorry to bother you."

She hung up. I went back to the Wash-o-matic to catch up on the overflow in the busing window. It took me way too long to realize that I should leave. That particular moment, that whole self-absorbed half-hour of me shuffling dishes and picking at tasty unfinished morsels of gourmet cuisine, more so than the rest of that dreadful day, will haunt me till the end.

I want it to haunt me till death. I was stuffing my face as Ana lay dying, as our fetus lay dying on the placenta.

After the dishes were caught up, I finally had the urge to leave and run to Ana. Her words hit me. I left unnoticed and sprinted to the house. Needless to say, I never worked another day at the Epicurean.

I ran like never before.

As for a supposed hero of myth, I might as well have been Hercules. Not the Hercules with his twelve feats and his superb pankration skills, but the Hercules that slaughtered his entire family from unjustified and insane anger, the cause of his obligatory feats.

I put it all on myself, the scene I came home to.

Ana was sprawled on the floor. There was blood all over the toilet.

I was trying not to panic. 'Never panic.' The words of my father.

Her hand-woven, cat-hair cloth was at her ankles, spotted with the red of life and death. I was saying her name over and over.

I was holding her head checking for a pulse. I was panicking. I remembered seeing her pulse times before on her carotid artery because she was so skinny and her skin was gossamer and pale. I checked her wrist.

Nothing.

I called 911.

Address?

Cause of Emergency?

"My girlfriend had a miscarriage. I think she's dead."

I looked in the toilet. A bunch of fleshy tissue swimming in dark red water. A prominent pink ovoid mass, a fetus in the 1 oz weight class wrestled the world and lost.

I was crying right away. I hadn't cried since the time I didn't make weight.

No pulse again.

"Please don't go. Stay here with me. I'm sorry. I'm sorry. Don't leave me for the underworld."

I pulled her Jain cloth up. How embarrassing for her. I looked back in the toilet at our baby. I was cleaning up the mess, the red toilet paper, crying. The spilt bottle of glucose pills.

I grabbed her up and held her.

I flushed it.

I don't know why.

The toilet clogged. The pink water rose to the top.

A waterfall of blood-soaked paper tissue and red human tissue and the dead miniature version of Ana and me spilled around us.

Chapter 26: Chthonic Journey

I was a silent observer of the busy scene of detectives and paramedics and coroners. I was Buddha under the Bo tree, Jesus in the desert. I was the *omphalos,* the navel of the universe, or I was the *omphaloskeptic,* the navel-gazer. I was the puked-up stone from Kronos, Father Time. I was the surrogate of his powerful son, his rejection of his demise. I was in shock and my tears were dried.

The cops asked me several questions. 'It's just protocol that we ask you these things. No one's accusing you of anything right now.' The female detective was sincere and motherly. She sat next to me.

I gestured to the yes/no questions, and all the answers I had to say aloud were barely sentences, mere phrases. I just wanted everyone and everything to go away. I wanted to punish myself, without pity. The pity I felt I did not deserve.

The female detective asked me one last question.

"Why did you try flushing it?"

I didn't know. I couldn't help but cry again, my hands over my face.

Hours passed and everyone left. I was still the Buddha, facing an army of my own personal fears and despair, but unlike him, they overwhelmed me. And unlike him, I had no will to leave my personal saturnine anguish.

I wasn't Jesus on the cross. Jesus did no wrong. I did everything wrong. My father did not forsake me, I forsook myself. I forsook Ana. I forsook our fetus.

David and Cy sat with me in silence. This was their way of consoling me. I appreciated it, but I felt I did not deserve the comfort.

I was Orpheus, I looked back at Hell and lost my lover's life to it, because of cowardice. And like him, I deserved a life of meandering torment and to be ripped apart limb from limb by zealous women.

I wanted to be Tantalus, who could never reach the fruit nor drink of the river. Forever starving, forever thirsty. Like him, I had sacrificed my child and tried to trick the Gods with my gourmet meal. I was the gluttonous deceiver, the blasphemer.

The house was dead calm and I hadn't moved, I was barely blinking. I finally chucked up some words.

"Could you buy me a bottle Cy?"

"Of course. What do you want?"

"Doesn't matter."

Cy left for the liquor store. David was on the floor cross-legged and drawing.

"I did this. Didn't I?" I said.

"No. Don't think that way. Ana chose her own path. You can't blame yourself for this." David said. He stopped drawing and looked at me. "This could have happened without you."

"I got her pregnant. This caused it all. That is all my fault." I said.

"You can't think like that. You couldn't have foreseen this." David said.

We fell silent again.

I wasn't Prometheus, I couldn't see the future. I didn't give humanity the gift of fire. I was the abuser of fire. The human with destruction in his hands who turns his back on God and all Gods. The coward defiler.

Saint Catherine said. 'Be who God intended you to be and you will set the world on fire.' She's right.

Cy got home and handed me a 1.75 liter bottle of whiskey. I thanked him and grabbed an egg from the refrigerator.

"I have to be by myself for awhile."

***

Whiskey comes from the Gaelic words for "water of life." This was the key to the gate of my *chthonic* journey. I wanted to be on my way to the Underworld. I wanted to be with Ana.

I broke the egg and spilled it into one of the snake-coiled clay cups. I sat on our mattress and poured myself some whiskey. The fiery taste didn't make me shutter. The burn on my throat was nothing to me. This was fire to Agni or Vulcan, lightning to Zeus or Indra.

I drank cup after cup of whiskey. The sun fell and the room got dark. I took my clothes off and tied on the *langot* that Ana had made me. I pulled out the lock of hair she gave and rubbed my cheek with it.

I started to cry. I balled like a baby on the bed in the fetal position. The *langot* might as well have been a diaper.

I calmed down and gazed around the room at all that made up the life I had with Ana. I lit one of her homemade candles. There were her posters, her *thinspiration* and her painting of Ana the Patron Saint of Infertility and the Mourner of the World's Suffering. The one who knew that if I became what God intended me to be, I would set the world on fire.

There was her loom in front of a stack of books. Next to it was her charkha on top of the wooden winebox that Sofia the soon-to-be-mummified cat was being stored in for the seventy day preservation period. Under that was another wooden winebox.

I looked inside the second box. In it were Ana's belongings, if you could say she owned anything, her diary and a bamboo quill with a bottle of ink. She had gotten these things from Devi, all made from scratch. There were also some sunflower seeds in a satchel, some dates, and a pomegranate. The diary's paper was handmade from reprocessing old newspapers and the binding was grass cordage. Devi made the ink herself from walnuts.

Written on the cover was *Anorexics' Cookbook.*

I opened it up and paged through it. A photograph fell out on the floor. I held it up to the candle to look. It was Ana the Ballerina. She was in a pirouette pose. She had to have been 14 or 15. She wasn't as thin as she was before she died. Written on the back of it was the word 'FATTY'.

I stared at the picture until the candle burned out. I was afraid of the diary. I couldn't bring myself to read any of it. I just drank and drank and cried.

I passed out in the fetal position.

I woke up as Tantalus, starving and thirsty, belly of void, mouth of drought. My head ached, good. Everything was spinning. I was in the maelstrom of the Cosmic Toilet. I was the *omphalos* in the spinning madness of the Universe proper. I was the *lingam* wrapped in the snake of creation at the brink of destruction.

The pain was such a small price to pay. I had my coins for Charon, I was ready for the ferry ride.

I didn't make it to the Underworld. Too cowardly for that, too weak-willed.

I crawled to the toilet and drank from it. Give me botulism, give me dysentery. Let me puke my brains out. Let me shit my guts out.

Let me die of thirst.

Let me starve to death.

I crawled to the cup with the raw egg in it. The salmonella bacteria had a whole night to colonize in that cup, like Europeans invading everywhere.

The rancid effluvium fazed me not. I drank it down. The yolk slid down my throat. Putrid rotten egg, colonized chicken fetus.

I did not flinch. I did not gag. Three cheers for the Underworld.

Life would not flash before my eyes. My life with Ana was like a slow motion movie in my head. Her face, her laugh, her smile. Those eyes and that mouth. She was my goddess. My Ana.

I crawled to the toilet and sat there. My abdomen was churning with razor blades, sharp cutting pains in the forefront of the raging fire of my stomach, Agni in my belly. Take me home, back to the tomb that once was a womb.

My bowels erupted and vomit burst forth with insane ferocity. My eyes were bulged. I aimed the puke between my legs. I didn't want to leave more than the mess of my death for someone to clean. I turned onto my knees to genuflect to the porcelain god. There was so much powerful liquid flow that I stuck my head into the toilet, flushing it all the while. A suicidal swirly, given to myself by the bully of myself, the bulimic oxen monster. Jacob the Clogged and Overflowing Toilet.

I was hot and sweating for a moment then freezing with powerful chills. My body convulsed against my mind's will.

I could barely get up and clean myself. I managed to get to the bed and after a few moments headed back to the toilet for more jettison episodes.

This was my life for three days. My body was getting rid of everything. Things I might have eaten long ago. I would not need a high colonic anytime soon. This was an all natural self-produced enema.

Those three days ran together with very little memory. I had been to the Underworld but did not stay. I was the cowardly Orpheus that wanted to live and wander the earth in melancholy.

My brother and David propped my head up and put a straw to my lips. I drank involuntarily there sweet acidic fluid, maybe watery lemonade. Sometimes it was daytime, sometimes night, sometimes on the threshold. By the fourth day, my abdomen was smoldering, the razors were gone. I was conscious of my surroundings.

I found the courage to read Ana's diary.

Chapter 27: Anorexic's Cookbook

She wrote all her thoughts and her poetry and songs. She documented every meal that she ate, calories and all. There wasn't a day skipped. On average, she was ingesting around 1500 to 1800 calories a day. I was confused. She ate very healthily. Fruits and nuts mainly, in all sorts of forms. None of it cooked though. These were habits of the Jains by eating only raw and unharvested food that she believed in. This explained her constant visits to Devi's house. What it didn't explain was how she didn't sustain her weight.

One entry explained where she went the day David and I stood under the bridge.

I made my decision. I'm keeping this baby. This being growing inside me is the product of mine and Jacob's love. I can't intentionally destroy that. I can't rationalize that with my own value system. It's a violent act. And though the sexual act is also a violent act, I feel justified in making love to Jacob still. This is one of the few violent acts I wish to keep. This and talking. I write my own rules. I created Ana and as a goddess, I can give her all the attributes I wish. Ana may be infertile, but I am obviously not. And I wish to live and strive with that. I would like to keep this beautiful soul we made. He or she or it will come to this world of agony with parents that will love them, teach and nurture them.

I walked the river as the ascetics do in India. I wanted to clear my head of my conflict with myself and with Jacob. I walked to the nearest abortion clinic to consult with myself. I stood across the street and watched the protesters with their signs of dead babies and fetuses. They didn't affect me in the least bit. How I used to hate them!

I consulted with the goddess within me. Ana represents non-violence and this should include this particular violent act. It's contradictory to my cause. The infertile cosmic daughter in me wants this baby and wants me to be a mother. I had to make the choice and I did. Jacob and I will bring this child into this world regardless of our personal suffering. We can be selfless guides for this being to walk this earth and show others that we do not need all this nonsense. We can live simple and pure.

I never want to burden anyone with my ailments, but I've been feeling constantly ill despite how much I've been eating. I do not feel nourished. I understand the morning sickness, but this feels like too much. I feel like I'm energized purely by spirit. All I want to do is sleep.

***

I really have to rid myself of my insecurities with my face. I have completed my self-security of my body, but I am still so brainwashed about my facial appearance. This is a mask I put on to hide myself from the world, to make myself look 'pretty'. Jacob thinks I am beautiful and he's all that matters.

Make-up has always been poison anyhow. The kohl that the Egyptians used gave them lead poisoning. The white basecoat which certain Renaissance aristocrats wore was laced with arsenic. The capitalist industry of modern make-up is highly poisonous to our society, for both men and women. I have to overcome this.

***

I have this compulsion to make myself a will in the case that I don't make it through this pregnancy or die during birth. I think I'll do this on my eighteenth birthday which is coming up soon. I believe dying is possible during childbirth considering how frail and weak I look and feel.

My requests are simple. I want to be cremated, and I want my half of my ashes to be kept with Jacob until our child is old enough to keep them. The other half I wish to be taken to the purest and most beautiful river in India. Devi knows where it is. I want my ashes to be spread on the ground and not in the river itself. I'm not vain enough to pollute any river, especially the river of life.

I hope that the family I would leave behind will depart this godforsaken country. Please do not give up. Be in this world. Help to change it. Help to make us better. Make us love!

I had thought about looking into having Jacob mummify me, but I honestly think that is egotistical and vain, just like tombs and the rest. Sure, it's a nice symbol when a cat is mummified, but as humans, we are nothing but walking and talking vanities of destruction. How I loathe are species! How I wish we could improve, spiritually evolve!

***

I have been thinking of taking a vow of silence again, until I give birth. Language is the pinnacle of us humans, and I understand that it does commit a great deal to the good half of human nature. But ultimately, given the base violence of the other half, I feel that language has been nothing but destructive to me and those around me. It is the source of all our conflicts. Whether it's with tribes that don't speak the same language and ultimately conquer each other or with lovers who misunderstand what they hear or say.

These conflicts with me and Jacob have been started by our inability to communicate. And we are both at fault. I'm not so full of myself to write otherwise.

***

There were many excerpts about me in Ana's diary. Some things were good and complimentary. But many were dissections of who I was and how I was being. All of these things were true. She wrote of my anger and destructive behaviors and my lack of communication. One section in particular was all about the binge eating she had suspected I had been doing at work. She could see it in my weight gain.

She had written psychological profiles about my issues with my father and my mother, Cy and David, and most extensively about herself.

She had listed ways in which she was dealing with her bipolar disorder, some of these being herbs that Devi had given her and *Kundalini* yoga.

She had drawn a picture of what she labeled as 'Symbol of Kundalini'. It was an egg with a snake coiled around it three and a half times. There was also a drawing of a whirlpool spinning around a pill shape.

The last entry was written the day before she died. It was her birthday. I was so self-absorbed I had never asked when her birthday was, and she never volunteered it. A twist of the knife I had put in my own back.

Ana's birthday present to herself was making her will. Her birthday present from me was a screaming tirade which sent her to her death.

Happy Birthday! I wanted someone to shoot me or hang me. I felt completely to blame for all of this.

Her last written words were this: *Jacob needs to find himself before he can be a good father. I really need to help him.*

Under it she wrote: *Ana always was, is, and always will be.*

This I know is true.

Chapter 28: Dust and Shadow

Dr. Pavlovich was sitting over me when I woke up on the seventh day after Ana's death. He was reading her book on Jainism. He was dressed in a black suit and his legs were crossed. There was a plate of fruit at his foot.

"She was a wonderful being, wasn't she?" He asked.

"The most." I said.

The room was stale and not as hot as it had been. Dr. Pavlovich studied me.

"Here, have some breakfast." He handed me the plate of food.

I took it and peeled a banana. Me, the simian survivor and spectator of Underworld goings on.

"We have much to talk about. So let me start with Ana's death." He said.

I didn't want to look at him. I could barely swallow a bite of banana. I drank some glucose water.

"She died of complications from anorexia as I know you suspect. She suffered from malnourishment which was the ultimate reason for her cardiac arrest. Your friend David told me that you are blaming yourself for her death, because you were drunk and yelling at her the night before and the day of. Stress may have sparked her miscarriage which triggered the cardiac arrest, but her long history of anorexia left her in a condition that put both the life of Ana and your child at risk. You can't blame yourself for that. Ana walked a razor's edge between morality and health. " Dr. Pavlovich said.

This did not make me feel relieved of anything. There was nothing to relieve the simple fact of loss, regardless of the reasons why. I would carry the guilt with me for the rest of my life.

"The mess surrounding Ana's death has been taken care of. There is not going to be a service for her. She had put this into her will along with very simple demands, one of them being, her request for cremation. She wanted you to have the ashes."

Dr. Pavlovich handed me a box that was sitting next to him. "A copy of the will is in the box. I would have bought an urn for you and her, but I figured you might want to pick out something yourself."

I looked him in the eyes. "Thanks for all of this."

"I'm honored to help. The legalities went very smoothly. Her foster family didn't want anything to do with it. They didn't want to pay for the cremation. This didn't surprise me. They were never interested in Ana anyway. They are rich spoiled brats who think they're winning at life, but they're faking it. They're truly rotten to the core. Helping people shouldn't be a part of a status symbol." He said.

"I no longer work for the FTC. I was part of a secret investigation to monitor the problems of these treatment facilities and their interactions with pharmaceutical companies and the government. My colleagues and I had been working at this for years and it finally came to a head. There are a lot of legal things to do for the next few years, but I thought you'd be interested that a small battle has been won against the corrupt money-hungry system of children's mental health. I'm personally glad to be out of the FTC. But that's enough about me. Let's talk about you. What are you going to do now?" He said.

"I haven't thought about any of that." I said.

"I'm going to help you, if you want my help." He said.

"I don't have much money."

"It's not like that Jacob. This is not about money. I'm not about money."

"I read your interview in Psychology Now." I said.

"Really? I'm impressed. That was back when I started this whole underground investigation on children's treatment facilities." He said. "Besides getting you back to good physical health, you have lots to do. You have to figure out some goals. I have a few reading suggestions for you that you need to get started on." He said and stood up. "You need to call your father and have a serious talk with him and tell him what you think."

"Why are you helping me?" I said.

"Your friend David called me. He thought I was the only one who could help with this situation, and besides, this is what I do, I help people."

"Thanks again."

"Don't think of it. Go home and see your mother. She brought you into this world and will forever love you no matter what. So go and tell her what you think and then you come see me."

Chapter 29: Jacob's Ladder

I listened to Dr. Pavlovich, my mentor, my guiding light through the dragon's cavern of tragedy.

I went home to see my mother. She was waiting for me on the couch in the living room, the house silent. She aged fifty years, it had been three months since the drive to FTC.

I hugged her. We cried. I was the baby in mommy's arms, the frail being that must survive, no, *live* in the world.

She couldn't talk, she mumbled how she loved me and how she prays for me.

"I'll be okay mom." I said.

"I shouldn't have sent you there." She said.

"It's fine."

We didn't talk about much. We never had much to talk about anyway. She never bothered me again about religion. She remained what she was when she brought me to the world, Mother the Nurturer, the Caregiver.

***

The summer was weakening. I spent the rest of it by the river mostly by myself, though David was always around somewhere, my silent vigil. I kept myself sustained on gathered nuts and plants from the river and Ana's garden and the occasional game that David had hunted with his sling. Nothing too much. I also continued to trade my labor with Devi for food and miscellaneous items.

I thought about the world and its end and Ana. Ana was my consciousness, my heart. Her heart was balanced even with the Feather of Truth, unlike mine or yours or a pharaoh's.

It took me weeks to tune and play anything melodious on the lyre. I strained to reconstruct the melodies of Ana's work songs. I couldn't match the songs note for note but came as close as I could remember. I wasn't Orpheus, my music and my voice was not made of mystical honey. I also played a version of my dad's song *Live in this world.* The three guitar chords that the song consisted of were not hard to translate on the lyre.

When I sang, I thought of Ana. When I ate, I thought of Ana. When I drank, I thought of Ana. When I did anything. Ana.

The time came for me to mummify Sophia. Devi had plenty of linen for me and David and I had collected and processed enough pine resin to mummify a human. I was afraid to start. I stared at the winebox contemplating the process. I paged through Herodotus' description. I had been avoiding alcohol because of my wellspring of sorrow, but I felt I needed the crutch to deal with Sophia's body. I needed 'spirits for my spirit.'

I cut the linen into strips. I wrapped the powdery dried and stiff body of Sophia with resin-dipped strips, layer by layer until I thought she was complete.

Her corpse lay in the sunshine, the pine resin drying. Her heart was in balance with the Feather of Truth. She did no wrong here on earth.

When Sofia was fully dried, I offered her to Judith the Catlady. She reluctantly accepted and kept it as a sentiment of Ana.

School started. Mercurial autumn was conquering the green of life with its blissful carriage of colorful death, fiery orange and vulcan red and gold eternal, under the marshmallow clouds sailing through the jovial blue sky.

I remained at my brother's house with him and David. We all wandered the house doing and making and fixing things. I tended and picked from Ana's garden which was across from the pankration pit. This was the peaceful symbol of Ana's cause, to *live* in the world without destroying it. Every day I looked at the sandpit, it became a full blown catbox.

I had no will to wrestle, no will to vomit. I tried purging my spirit of my guilt and misery which pinned me to this earth. I could not be free of it. The Greeks called it *kenosis,* or emptiness. It was written that Jesus emptied himself. Epicuris made himself nothing. Buddha left the miserable cycle. Never was I, nor would be, fully shed of my grief. I was to walk this earth as Orpheus in the irreconcilable anguish.

At school, I walked through the halls in the congested flow of people I had known. They knew me no more. I was what my dad said Native Americans' call being 'touched'. I was accursed with tragedy. I had the aura of plight from the cosmic heart of the abyss. I did not smell of the Garden of Eden like Biblical Jacob. I smelled of death, the Stygian underbelly of the living.

People talked of me, never to me, and I didn't care. When I told my wrestling coach that I wasn't going to wrestle my final season, he never asked why. He *knew*. I tried my best to succeed at all of my classes, I still had my mom and brother and friend to be proud of me for something.

When school ended, it was time for me to leave. I packed my Survival Rucksack, my basic survival tools and food rations, the red *langot* and grass bracelet, Ana's diary with her picture and lock of hair, and Ana herself. Also strapped to my rucksack was my lyre. I was to walk the earth and find the cleanest river in India to spread Ana's ashes.

David wanted so badly to come with me, but he knew that this was my path of my atonement and that I must go alone. 'We'll meet again in the world my friend.' He told me and handed me a scroll marked with my name written in Hebrew. 'Read it when you're on your path.'

Cy didn't have much to say besides telling me to watch my back and call him if I needed anything. He gave me a few things from his Survival Rucksack and told me to "Go with God". No shit-eating grin at all.

My mother and I had very little to talk about. She said she loved me and told me 'God be with you.' She meant it.

I spent a day with Dr. Pavlovich. He gave me as much insight as he felt he should. He knew the purpose of my journey and felt it right for my person.

"Know Thyself. That is the other ancient advice written near the *Omphalos*." He told me.

We talked about Ana and he shared with me all the things that he knew of her from the years of counseling. Most of it I knew, but I liked hearing anything about Ana, she was all I thought about anyway.

I talked with Devi about India and where I should go. She made us tea and we talked for a while.

"Sadly Jacob, there are no more clean rivers in India anymore, just sections. Industrialization and overpopulation has brought an imbalance to all the rivers. But I do know of the river Ana would choose. It is the Yamuna River. This is the goddess Yamuna, she is the daughter of the sun god Surya and the Dawn goddess Saranyu. Her brother is Yama, the god of death. The sections I know that are cleanest are closest to the head of the river near the feet of the Himalayas." Devi said.

She gave me some supplies, my own diary and ink, a list of phone numbers of friends and family that she had in India that could help me.

***

David's scroll read:

Jacob and Ana stand at the Heart of Heaven on the Kingdom of Earth.

The Crown surrounds the Union of the Two, One perfect ring around Life.

Jacob stands at the Ladder below the Heart of Heaven.

Jacob rests his head on the rock, the Earth, the Kingdom.

The Place where God meets Man. The Gate.

Jacob the Conduit of Celestial light, the Sun with Rays for rungs, climbs through the Gate.

The vision of God as All.

And as None.

Unthinkable, Unknowable, Eternal aspect of Self and Selfless.

Jacob heals his heart with the divine dreams of dynamic balance
On the central stone of the World
He unlocks the Silver Lock on the Heart of Heaven
And lets Ana go forth to the Center of God
Where the void is full and fullness is void.

***

My first stop was Alaska to see my father. The days and weeks went by like water. I walked and hitchhiked through America and Canada. I played my lyre wherever I was stationary, most times I got enough money to buy food, sometimes not. My stomach had hardened, an iron shield of my rebirthing spirit. I wasn't bothered in the least to have an empty belly, I just thought of Ana and walked on.

I stayed for a short time with my dad in Alaska. He saw I was 'touched' the moment I arrived at his commune. He wasn't drunk, he was expecting me. He hadn't changed either, the same tough as nails eschatologist that left us two years prior.

He had taken up beekeeping and was more serious with it than anything else, even the wine and liquor making.

He told me a quote from Einstein. "If the bee disappears from the surface of the earth, man would have no more than four years to live."

We didn't talk about Ana or my mother or anything of what happened to me, but he did tell me a story I had never heard about him and his friend in Vietnam. We were both drunk on the mead he made from the honey of his bees. We sat around a fire and I was plucking my lyre and he said at the end of the story, "and they gave me a medal for watching my friend's head get shot off."

He cried.

Until then, I had never seen my father cry, never ever.

When I felt it was my time to leave, he decided to come with me to make sure I could get on a ship to cross the Pacific.

We were at the port, it was raining.

"Live in the world son, not in the next." My dad said.

"You too dad, you too."

I realized what he meant by his song. He was advising me to do what he couldn't do. He could not live in the world of today. He was living in the world of tomorrow and of yesterday just like the people he despised that live for the hereafter.

I was to live in the world, in the now. Not the next world, not the past, not tomorrow.

Live now.

***

Across the world and years, I walked with my lyre and sang Ana's songs in the key of my grief. By ship and car and bus and foot I slowly made my way to India. I wanted Ana to be with me everywhere I went until I was at peace with letting her go.

Wherever I saw a form of wrestling or boxing, I stopped to watch or when I was allowed, participate. Karate and Jujitsu and Sumo in Japan. Kung Fu and Shuai Jiao in China. Thai boxing in Thailand. And when I got to India I found a Pehlwani school along my way to the head of the Yamuna. I got to wrestle in my *langot* with some of the hardest trained wrestlers I had ever come across.

I followed the Yamuna River, the River Goddess, all the way towards the head. Days went by like blinks. There were no McMill's selling toys with poisonous food. There was no Santomon genetically modifying plants covered in the same poison eaten at McMill's. There was no Proxy and Keno with their psycho-drugs for the whole family, no chemical omnicidal cleaners to sterilize plastic houses.

There were no toilets.

I walked, my brain as fluid and steady as the singing Yamuna river next to me.

Where the river was the cleanest, I walked along and little by little scattered Ana's ashes.

I remembered what Ana had told me about the sanctity of long walks and how walking cleanses the spirit. And if one walked long enough, one could be emptied of grief.

I climbed and climbed into the light air up the ladder where the earth meets the heavens.

The mountains, my rungs. The river, its fluid steady voice, my conduit. The sky, my canopy of change.

I slept under my tarp and spontaneous rain or in the earthy air of a shallow cave. I made small fires when the trees were abundant. Next to each fire, I played Ana's songs. I plucked tender notes on the lyre strings, the cured bowels of Sophia. I sang to Ana's family and they sang with me, her mother earth and father sky, her river sister and tree sister, and to all of her sibling creatures that inhabit the world. It was time for her to be with them, in this world, not the next.

I emptied myself of grief, purged it, I heaved my torment into heaven and flushed it away.

I didn't cry next to the river, I didn't have to. I had cried enough.

I was at peace with death, full of life.

Ana lives on the riverbank with her true family.

She lives in them and with them, the animals, the plants, the tree, the fruit, the seed.

She lives there, in the mountains, the rivers, the oceans, the earth and universe.

Ana lives inside me, in my heart.

Ana is everywhere.

ABOUT THE AUTHOR

Ivan Wayne Baker lives in Milwaukee, Wisconsin where he writes and edits. He also both plays and coaches hurling and boxing, likes backpacking and camping, cooking and brewing, and most of all enjoys time with his kids and wife, family and friends.

For a peek at his next upcoming novel go to:

dipso.wordpress.com

Find news about the author on these websites:

www.threefacedmedia.com

www.ivanwaynebaker.com

Photo by Irma Roman

Made in the USA
Charleston, SC
18 May 2013